BLACK MAGIC

Edgar Waldgrave

BLACK
MAGIC

The Witch Chronicles

Rise of the Dark Witch High King

Book Two

Hometown Publishers

Hometown Publishers
www.hometownpublishers.com

First Published by Hometown Publishers July, 2020.

ISBN: 978-1-7770337-4-3 (Paperback)
ISBN: 978-1-7770337-5-0 (E-book)

Library and Archives Canada (LAC) national library collection.

Cover Design by Edgar Waldgrave.

Dedication

To B, D,

J, & M

To my dad and mom,

C & M

Acknowledgements

Thank you for reading my fictional account

of The Witch Chronicles as they pertain to

the White, Gray, Black, and Dark Witches

of the Northeast Region of the United States.

Please note that the towns of Thornton,

Onondaga County, Charlotte, Cayuga County,

and the village of Dockside, Onondaga County,

even though described and geographically

portrayed as being in the State of New York,

are fictitious.

Thank you to all the people and establishments,

in the eleven Northeast States in the USA.

Enjoy...

Chapter One

"Al, you're hurting me," pleaded Jane as she was pulled by the hair from the living room into the kitchen, her face all bloodied, and right eye swollen.

"I'm just getting warmed up, bitch," warned Al, throwing her down on the wooden floor.

"You're drunk, please, just let me leave," she begged. "You can sleep it off and I'll be back in the morning to make you breakfast." Jane knew once she got out the front door, she was never coming back, but the door looked a million miles away.

"I'm not even close to drunk yet," he replied, opening the half empty bottle of vodka, and taking a good, long swig. "And since when, do you tell me what to do?" he asked, with a hard kick to her ribs, resulting in the echoing sound of two of them cracking like dry wood on a fire.

Jane buckled on the floor in pain; she knew if she didn't get out of that house, she was dead.

Al sat on the kitchen chair, and in between gulps of vodka, pointed and laughed at her.

Jane patiently waited till he finished the bottle. "Here baby, let me get another one for you," she said slowly getting off the floor. The pain in her side was excruciating but she managed to reach for the cupboard door, open it, and grab a full bottle of vodka. Her plan was to swing around, hit him over the head with it, and make for the door. But before she could, he was standing right behind her, and grabbed it.

"If I didn't know any better," he slurred, "I would say you were thinking about cracking this over my head."

"No, Al," she lied, "I would never hurt you; I love you."

Al laughed out loud. "That's a good one, my slut of a wife loves me…plus, every other man in this town she's slept with."

"I've never been with anyone else," she said honestly, "you know I would never do that to you."

Al turned away from her and went towards the chair. Jane realized it was now or never. With all her might she pushed Al forward causing him to fall and bang his head off the side of the kitchen table. Jane fell next to him and started to crawl. She had made it to the living room, when suddenly a hand grabbed her leg, pulling her back. She looked up at Al standing over her with blood streaming down the side of his face.

"You are going to pay for that you little bitch!" he shouted, and with both hands lifted the bottle of vodka over his head, with the intent of coming down hard and splitting her skull with it.

Jane quickly got onto her knees, and with a hard, fast right uppercut, connected directly with his testicles. Al dropped to the floor gasping. Jane shakily got off her knees, balanced herself on the wall, and slowly staggered to the front door. She was feeling dizzy, blood was streaming into her eyes, and she desperately wanted to sit down and rest; but she knew if she did, she would never get back up. "Come on Jane, you need to keep moving, or else he is going to grab you again," she said motivating herself. Jane zigzagged out the door, made her way gradually down the steps onto the front path, and crossed the street to Lisa and Ted's house, and knocked.

"Where did you go bitch?" yelled Al from the front door. "I'm going to get you for that!"

Lisa looked out her front window, saw the condition of her friend, and heard Al yelling across the street. She left the porch lights off, quietly opened the door, and gently helped Jane in.

"I'll get you tomorrow," he whispered going inside, slamming the door, and picking up his bottle of vodka from the floor. "It must be my lucky day," he mumbled smiling at it, "you're still in one piece." He removed the cap and took a big mouthful. "I think I'll finish you off in bed," he declared as he started to sluggishly climb the stairs. All of a sudden, a black cat meowed, and darted past his legs. "Magic, is that you?" he asked.

Al eventually made it to the top of the landing and turned on the light. The black cat suddenly leapt out of the darkness with a high-pitched scream, startling Al, and causing him to stumble backwards to the top of the stairs. Al had almost regained his balance, but the cat jumped onto his chest, shifting his weight, and causing him to fall. The cat swiftly jumped onto the landing, watched Al tumble down the stairs, and listened to the sound of his bones cracking. The last snap, the loudest sound of all, was his neck breaking. The black cat leisurely sauntered down the stairs, crawled onto Al's chest, and stared into his vacant eyes. Then sprang onto the living room floor and scuttled to the open window. Once outside, the cat crossed the road, went through the neighbors' yards, and headed for home.

Chapter Two

Monday, July 6

"Mr. Blake, I have to say, that was a lovely service you had for your great-uncle," said Mr. Donaldson offering him a seat.

"Thank you," he replied, "and please, call me Andrew."

"Andrew," he said sitting on the opposite side of the large mahogany desk, "your great-uncle was well-liked in this town, not only by his parishioners but the townspeople in general, and he will be sorely missed."

"That's most kind of you to say."

Sean gave him a quick smile then picked up his paperwork and got down to business. "As his attorney, I helped your great-uncle write his final will a few months ago, and as you are aware, you are the only surviving relative. So, everything has been left to you. This includes: his house, the furnishings, his personal possessions, and his car. He also had money in a personal bank account, which has been withdrawn, and a check made out to you. Along with a sizeable life insurance policy, which you are also the beneficiary of." Sean looked up at Andrew. "Although I pointed out that you are the only surviving member, your great-uncle was extremely fond of you, and spoke about you constantly and with the utmost admiration."

"He was a very kind and caring man," responded Andrew.

"That he was," said Sean genuinely, before flipping through his pages. "The house and land are in excellent condition. If you are planning on selling the property, I don't believe you will have a difficult time finding a buyer who will pay top dollar, and if that is something you are considering, please let me know, and I can help you out," he suggested, then thought about another viable option, and glanced up. "Or maybe you are planning on keeping it?"

"I am, for the time being," answered Andrew. "I thought I would take the summer to go through his personal effects and decide in the fall."

"That's understandable, take as much time as you need," said Sean empathetically. "There's no rush, and this town is beautiful in the summer…but of course, you already know that."

"Yes," replied Andrew good-naturedly.

"Now," said Sean getting back to the task at hand. "Over the last two weeks, I did escort a group of cleaning ladies into your great-uncle's home to remove any garbage, spoilt food from the fridge, and conduct some surface cleaning. Trust me, nothing was removed I assure you. I just didn't want you, upon your return, to walk into a…" said Sean stopping and searching for the right word.

"No need to explain, it was very thoughtful, and I appreciate you doing that for me."

"You're welcome," said Sean with a gratifying nod before removing some papers from his file. "If I can just get your signature on these forms," he said passing them over, "here, here, and here." He watched Andrew sign them then took them from him. "Here are the keys to the house, and these are for the car," he clarified before handing them over. "These two small keys your great-uncle gave to me a few weeks ago. He told me they were extremely important and that it was imperative I gave them to you directly," he explained removing them from an envelope and placing them in Andrew's hand. "I have no idea what they are for, but he said that you would."

Andrew looked at them carefully and shook his head mystified.

"Maybe they're for a desk drawer or cabinet?" suggested Sean before continuing. "Here is the check from your great-uncle's bank account, and this one is from his insurance company."

Andrew's eyes widened when he read the second amount.

Sean smiled at his reaction. "He told me he wanted you to be taken care of," he said in a friendly tone, "and he hoped this would help."

Andrew thought momentarily about his great-uncle, and how much he missed him, before reestablishing eye contact with Sean.

"Of course, nothing can replace him, he was a wonderful man," consoled Sean noticing the sadness in Andrew's eyes.

"No," whispered Andrew giving him a distant look.

Sean, sensing Andrew's sorrow, quickly wrapped things up. "Before we conclude our business, do you have any questions?"

"None," answered Andrew shaking his head.

"Okay, then we are all done here," confirmed Sean.

"Thank you for everything," replied Andrew standing and following him to the door.

"Oh! I almost forgot to tell you about your next-door neighbors," stated Sean, pausing briefly to think about how Andrew's house was situated. "When you walk out your front door, your neighbor to your left," he said motioning with his left hand, "is the new receptionist at the church. Actually, she's been working there for over a year now, and knew your great-uncle quite well. She's a spinster, and is usually at the church throughout the day, and tends to keep to herself most evenings. To your right, is a young lady who moved in about a month ago, and come September, she will be teaching at the State Street Elementary School up in Skaneateles. They are both wonderful people and ideal neighbors, and I'm sure they will drop by, and say hello."

"I look forward to meeting them," acknowledged Andrew pleasantly.

"If you have any questions, or if there is anything you need, please don't hesitate to contact me," said Sean reaching out and shaking Andrew's hand.

"I will, and again, thank you for everything."

"It's been my pleasure," replied Sean. "Welcome to Thornton."

Chapter Three

Andrew was busy unpacking when he heard a knock at the door, and went downstairs, and opened it.

"Hi, I'm your neighbor from next door," said the attractive blonde.

"Hello," he replied, "my name is Andrew."

"Hello, Andrew, I'm Gwyneth, but everyone calls me Gwyn. Except my old aunt May, who still likes to call me Gwynnie, and refuses to ignore my long-standing protest to her calling me that," she clarified nervously.

"Well, it's nice to meet you, Gwyn."

"Oh, these are for you," she said, handing him a twelve pack of Budweiser. "A welcome present of sorts…I know neighbors traditionally drop off a pie or dinner, but unfortunately, I didn't have time today, maybe tomorrow," she suggested, feeling a little embarrassed.

"Beer is perfect, my great-uncle wasn't a beer drinker so there's none here, and I was planning on picking some up later," he explained, "but you've saved me the trip. Would you like to come in and have one?"

"I'd love to," she replied, happy that he had offered.

Andrew put the case on the coffee table, opened two, and gave her one.

"How's the place coming along?" asked Gwyn looking around. "Looks like you have everything well-organized."

"To be honest with you, I only brought clothes, these furnishings are either my great-uncle's or his parents."

"Really!" she said surprised. "I heard you were moving here so I just assumed some of this stuff was yours too," she said feeling awkward and giggling anxiously.

Andrew laughed with her. "Don't worry about it, if I had moved some of my stuff into this place, it would have looked like a disaster zone."

Gwyn curiously wandered around the living room. "Are you going to keep it like it is?"

"For now," he replied. "I'm planning on spending the summer going through his personal effects, and what I do with the furnishings will depend on whether I sell it or not."

"So, you're thinking about selling the house?"

"I'm not sure. I have a place in Syracuse, and I work around the corner at the university part time, so it's handy and close to downtown. I also teach a couple of courses at Cortland, which is only a thirty-minute drive."

"That does sound nice, and convenient."

"It is, but I love visiting here, which is why I'm unsure," he clarified. "Would you like to sit?"

"I would, thank you," she replied taking a seat on the couch. "What is it that you do at the colleges?"

"I'm a professor, I teach criminology, part time," he replied sitting in the armchair next to her.

"Not full time?" she asked.

"No, I like having some time off to run, read, and when I get the chance, write fictional detective novels."

"Detective novels, that's interesting," she said tilting forward toward him. "Have you published any?"

"I finally got my first one published last year, and this summer, I'm starting on my next."

"How exciting!" she said with a cute smile. "Are you going to write about here?"

"Maybe," he replied tentatively.

Gwyn quickly realized his hesitation. "I'm so sorry, how thoughtless of me to ask such a question when you have other personal priorities to attend to."

"It's okay, I don't mind talking about it, it helps take my mind off other things," he said reassuringly and giving her an amiable smile. "Truth is, I really haven't decided the setting yet, which is the main reason for me being vague."

"Maybe this town will decide for you," replied Gwyn feeling a little more relaxed. "What made you want to study criminology?"

"My father was a detective, and I guess at one point I seriously considered following in his footsteps, but realized I would prefer to teach and write about it rather than live it."

"And was he okay with that?"

"He was, actually both my parents were," he said candidly. "They understood being a detective in the city is hard work, with long hours, and can take a toll on a person and his family."

"Is he still a detective or did he retire?"

Andrew went quiet.

"I apologize. I'm bombarding you with one personal question, after another," she said apprehensively, then sipped her beer.

Andrew looked at her, there was something about her naturalness that made him feel comfortable. He had never spoken openly about his parents, not even to his closest friends, but for some reason he wanted to be with her. "My parents died in a car accident six months ago," he said in a low voice.

"I'm so sorry," she said sympathetically. "Do you mind me asking what happened?"

"No," he replied slowly. "There was heavy snow falling, causing whiteouts along the interstate. A tractor trailer had jackknifed and the cars approaching couldn't see it, resulting in a thirty-car pileup, and a lot of casualties."

"I remember hearing about that on the news, back in January," said Gwyn sadly. "It was awful."

"It was the worst day of my life," said Andrew despondently.

Gwyn felt terrible. "I'm not doing too good with my, 'Welcome, I'm your next-door neighbor conversation.' First, I ask about you writing a story here when you still have things to sort out with your great-uncle, and now, your parents. I'm zero for two, I think I should just quit talking. Besides, I've ran out of feet to put into my mouth."

Which made Andrew laugh, then Gwyn.

"Don't worry about it, I haven't even talked to some of my closest friends about my parent's death," he said reassuring her. "Consider us discussing it a good thing for me, okay?"

"I will," she replied feeling more at ease, and happy with the fact that he felt comfortable enough around her to be so open.

"You moved here a month ago?" asked Andrew changing the subject.

Gwyn covered her mouth as she snickered.

Andrew looked at her puzzled.

"I didn't mean to laugh, you just caught me off guard, I thought you knew already."

"I knew what?" he asked curiously.

"My parents own the house I'm living in, I grew up there, well, up until I was thirteen. Then my father got a job with a firm in the city, we moved there, and that's where I went to high school and college, SU," she said with a smile. "My mom's only condition before we moved away was that we keep the house here, and we come up on the occasional weekends, at Christmas, and in the summer. So, when I was growing up, that's what we did."

"How would I have known all that?" asked Andrew chuckling. "Mr. Donaldson only said you moved in a month ago."

"That's true, I did," she replied. "But he didn't tell you the rest?"

"No," he replied shaking his head.

"Now you're wondering why he didn't at least say, I was moving back home, rather than I had just moved here?"

"I am," said Andrew intrigued.

"Sean and my father are old friends. If he would have told you my family's history, when I dropped by to say hello, I would have had nothing to talk to you about."

Andrew laughed aloud. "So you told him not to tell me?"

"Maybe," she said ambiguously and playfully looked away. Her first instincts were right, he was nice, and she liked him. "You know, I went to your great-uncle's funeral."

"You did," said Andrew surprised. "I'm sorry for not saying thank you earlier, it's just that I don't remember seeing you there."

"There's no need to apologize, there were a lot of people, and I'm sure it was a very difficult day for you," she said compassionately. "It was a lovely ceremony; for a lovely man."

"You knew him?"

"I did," she replied. "When my mother was growing up here, she knew his parents better, because your great-uncle was away at college, then at the seminary. She only met him when he would come home and visit. I also met him then, but I was very young, and soon after we moved away," she explained. "I really got to know him more when he lived here, and we came back to visit. He was always kind, gentle, and so easy to talk to."

"He was all those things," agreed Andrew.

"He spoke of you all the time," she said with a gentle smile.

"Not only was he my great-uncle, but a good and dear friend," said Andrew thinking about him. "He took me under his wing and helped me through an extremely difficult time in my life, and we became very close."

Gwyn reached out and squeezed Andrew's hand. "I know you miss him…I do, too…we all do. He was very well thought of in Thornton," she said before letting go.

"I'm glad to have someone to talk to about him," said Andrew liking her more and more.

"Anytime," she replied. "I'm right next door."

"Oh great, thanks for reminding me!" joked Andrew, lightening up the conversation.

"Hey, watch it mister!" she warned mischievously.

Andrew laughed, finished his beer then stood up and grabbed the case. "I'll put the rest in the fridge and grab us another," he said starting to walk away, and then turned around. "Are you coming?"

Gwyn happily followed Andrew into the kitchen, took a beer from him, and watched him put the remainder away before closing the door. "I'm free tomorrow, if you want me to go to the grocery store with you?" she asked with an innocent look.

"Are you referring to my empty fridge?"

"I am," she replied with a giggle.

Andrew proceeded to show her the bare cupboards and pantry, before telling her about the women coming in, and removing the food and cleaning up.

"That was nice of them."

"I thought so, too," he replied, then took a sip of his beer. "I was going to order pizza tonight. If you don't have any plans, you are more than welcome to join me?"

"I would like that," she replied reaching for her phone, dialing, and waiting. "I know the perfect pizza place," she whispered, with a frolicsome smile, then covered her phone, "actually, it's the only pizza place in town!"

They went outside, sat on the porch swing, and waited for it to arrive. Suddenly, an elderly lady appeared from around the corner startling them.

"Good evening, Mrs. Peabody," said Gwyn standing and walking towards her.

"Please Gwyn, call me Lenore, you make me sound like an old woman," she said slowly walking up the steps. "Hello, Andrew, I'm Lenore Peabody, your neighbor. I'm also a volunteer receptionist at the church."

"Happy to meet you, Lenore," said Andrew politely as he stood next to Gwyn.

"I won't take up too much of your time and will get right to the point. I was hoping you would like to come over for lunch tomorrow, say around one?"

"I would like that, thank you."

"You are more than welcome too, Gwyn, if you're not busy?" she said looking at her.

"Thank you, I would love to."

Out of the darkness, a black cat crept up the steps, and started brushing up against Andrew's calves, surprising him.

"Oh my!" said Lenore. "Magic usually doesn't take to strangers so quickly, but I see he's quite fond of you."

Andrew crouched down and stroked the cat as it lay on its side and purred.

"Well, I think Magic has found a new best friend," she said before starting back down the steps. When she reached the bottom, she turned around and reconfirmed, "one o'clock, sharp," then disappeared around the corner.

Andrew looked at the cat then at Gwyn. "Magic's not going to go with Lenore?" he asked sitting down next to it and rubbing its belly.

"No, Magic is an outdoor cat, practically everyone in town knows him," she said taking a seat next to them. "During the day, he stays close to home, and just lies around soaking in the sun, but at night, he's seen all around town, he's quite the traveler."

Chapter Four

"I really enjoyed last night," said Gwyn meeting Andrew, who was sitting on his front porch step. "It's been a long time since I've talked with someone so openly, it's refreshing."

"As you were approaching, I was just thinking the same thing," he said with a smile as he stood and walked with her. "How well do you know Lenore?"

"Not that well, in fact, I hardly know her. If she's not at the church, she tends to keep to herself at home. I guess a lot of people her age, are like that."

Andrew knocked on the door and it quickly opened.

"Right on time," said Lenore pleasantly. "Please, come in."

They followed her into what she called the parlor and offered them a seat on the couch while she stood over them. "Now, I wonder what you would like in your tea?" she asked studying them. "Gwyn, I'm guessing milk, no sugar, and Andrew, milk, with one sugar."

"That's right," said Gwyn, impressed.

"Mine also," confirmed Andrew, equally impressed.

"When you have been drinking and serving tea as long as I have, you get a knack for sizing people up quite quickly. Me, I only drink cream with my tea, I don't like milk," she revealed, then headed towards the kitchen before turning around. "Please, feel free to look around."

Andrew and Gwyn walked over to the wall and admired the paintings. Then moved down to the mantel, and looked at a picture of Lenore when she was a child with her parents, and another one with her grandparents, before walking over to the bookshelf.

Andrew read some of the titles out loud, "'Salem Witch-Hunt,' 'Magic, Spells, and Potions,' 'The Modern Witch,' 'History of Wiccans,' 'Ailuranthropy,'" then stopped and looked over at Gwyn's bewildered, wide-eyed face.

"I see you have taken an interest in my books," said Lenore, carrying a tray and placing it on the coffee table. "Come, sit," she said as she poured the tea. "Please, help yourself to a side plate and a sandwich."

As they ate and drank, Lenore looked over at her bookshelf and back at the couple sitting on the couch. "I was born in Salem, my parents were born and raised there, and I lived there till I was twenty. Salem has such a history of witches, wiccans, and ghosts, and every household you visit has books upon books on the subject. Most of those over there are my mother's, and given to her, by her mother. There are a few that I have bought, specifically on the topic of modern-day witches, they are quite amusing but nothing more," she explained, sipping her tea. "I only keep the older ones because of the sentimental value."

"It's nice to keep heirlooms around you," said Gwyn, "it reminds you of who you are, where you came from, and to be thankful for what you have today."

"Very nicely put, my dear," said Lenore with an approving smile.

"I noticed you have paintings of Plymouth and Sandwich in Massachusetts?" queried Andrew.

"Yes, after we left Salem, we lived in Boston for a number of years, then I lived in Plymouth for several years with my grandparents, and then with my aunt and uncle in Sandwich for quite a few years. After that, I started travelling," she said quietly. "Salem was nice enough but a little too spooky for me," she admitted looking over at the paintings. "I think Sandwich was my favorite place. Maybe one day, I will return there, and live out the rest of my days," she said with a sigh. "In the meantime, I'm quite content here."

"Sandwich, named after the seaport in Kent, England," said Andrew.

"You know your history," said Lenore, intrigued.

"I spent several summers in Cape Cod, around Peter's Pond, not too far from the town."

"I know that area very well," replied Lenore. "Do you know what the fourth Earl of Sandwich, John Montagu, is famous for inventing?"

"I do," replied Andrew smiling, "the sandwich."

"Really?" asked Gwyn, unconvinced.

"He's quite right dear," said Lenore, picking up a plate. "Here, have another one of his ingenious inventions," she said as she watched them each take a sandwich. After they finished, she poured more tea, and offered them shortbread cookies.

Magic appeared and made his way slowly to the couch, then effortlessly jumped up, and nestled in Andrew's lap.

"Well, I've never seen him do that before," said Lenore clasping her hands happily. "Is he bothering you? I can remove him if you like?"

"No, he's fine," said Andrew stroking the purring cat.

Lenore shook her head in dismay, then proceeded to tell them that after she left Sandwich, she travelled from town-to-town meeting fascinating people, experiencing different cultures, and enjoying life. "It has been such a pleasure meeting so many wonderful people, I truly feel blessed."

"Is it difficult to leave a town?" asked Gwyn.

"Yes and no," she replied. "Yes, in so much as I will miss the people; but no, because I know I am going to meet other interesting individuals, such as you two." Lenore quickly looked over at the clock on her mantel. "Oh my, look at the time," she said standing. "I hate to rush you out like this, but I need to be at the church before four, that's when confessions begin."

Andrew placed Magic on the couch, then stood with Gwyn, and waited for Lenore to return from dropping the tray off in the kitchen, before walking with her to the front door.

"Thank you both for coming," she said sincerely." It's so nice to chat with such fine, young people."

"Thank you," they replied.

"This is for you, a welcome gift," said Lenore, handing Andrew a pecan pie. "I baked it fresh this morning."

"That's very kind of you," said Andrew graciously.

"Gas baked pies always seem to taste that much better than conventional ovens do," she said opening the front door.

Andrew and Gwyn said goodbye, went out onto the porch, and headed home.

"She's a lovely woman," said Gwyn. "I know she has quite a few church friends, but she seems lonely, like she misses having a family."

"I think you're right," said Andrew looking over at her. "I got the feeling all her family has passed on, which may explain why she travels so much, and wants to meet new people."

Chapter Five

"This is the last of the groceries," said Andrew walking into his kitchen and placing them on the table. "It's almost seven, what do you want to do for dinner?"

"Well, you have dessert," said Gwyn motioning towards the pecan pie, "and this morning I made lasagna for us," the 'us' slipping out. "I meant for you, but I thought if you didn't want to eat it alone, I could join you," she explained awkwardly. "You know what. I'll just go and get it," she said leaving.

Andrew chuckled as he followed her to the door.

"So, you think my 'us' blunder is humorous?"

"Yes, I do, and very cute," he replied. As he opened the door, Magic darted in and sprang up onto his chest, making him stagger backwards. Gwyn reactively grabbed Andrew's arm, to stabilize him, and stop him from falling.

"The poor thing looks terrified," said Gwyn caressing the cat and trying to calm it down.

"That makes two of us," said Andrew, as Magic purred and snuggled into his chest.

Gwyn took her hand away from the cat and stroked Andrew's hair. "There, there, you feel better now?" she asked impishly.

Andrew purred and rubbed his head against her hand.

Gwyn giggled at his antics as she removed it and strolled out the door. Five minutes later she returned and heard Andrew in the kitchen.

"Glass of wine?" he asked.

"Please," she replied. "I just need to warm this up," she said placing the lasagna on top of the stove and turning the oven on, before taking the glass of wine from him. "Where's your buddy?"

"After I put him down, he jumped onto the couch" explained Andrew. "He's not there?"

"I don't know, I didn't notice him, but then again, I didn't really look. I just assumed he would still be clinging onto you," she said teasingly.

Emma opened the windows in the living room and let the warm breeze blow the drapes softly in the air as she walked up the stairs to the bathroom. Once there, she opened the window slightly, and turned on the bathwater. She poured a capful of milk, mixed with seven drops of pure lavender, into the falling water, and momentarily watched the oil disperse around the tub. Then opened a bottle of wine and poured a half glass, before lighting several scented candles. She removed her robe and admired her body in the door-length mirror. Cheerleading and gymnastics from her youth, and her daily exercise program, had kept it fit and tight. She leaned in and looked at her attractive face then stood back. Without this body and this face, she thought, she would never be able to do what she did; they were her meal ticket. She turned the water off, picked up her glass, and slipped into the bath. As she sipped her wine, she closed her eyes and thought about what she was going to do tonight, something very special. All of a sudden, the sound of purring made her open her eyes, and look over the side of the tub. "Hey, Magic, what brings you up here?"

Magic meowed back.

"Are you hungry, girl?"

Followed by another meow.

"Why don't you jump up here onto the toilet lid and wait till I'm finished, then I will get you some tuna. How does that sound?"

Magic leapt onto the lid, sat, and watched Emma as she drank her wine and closed her eyes.

Minutes later, the sound of the hairdryer startled Emma. She sat up and looked over at Magic standing next to it. "Wait, what?" asked Emma, wondering how the black cat had turned it on.

Magic slowly pawed the hairdryer towards the bath.

Emma suddenly realized what the cat was doing. "No, Magic," she shouted, "naughty cat!"

Magic pushed the hairdryer a couple more times. It was teetering on the edge of the shelf.

Emma looked on in horror and screamed, "No! Please no!"

Magic gave it one last push.

The hairdryer hit the water, the lights in the bathroom blinked rapidly off and on, as the electrical current ran through the water and Emma's body. Emma twitched for several moments then stopped. The black cat jumped down onto the toilet lid, stared into Emma's vacant eyes, and left.

"I must say that lasagna was delicious," complimented Andrew, "and the company has been delightful."

"Thank you, thank you," said Gwyn. "I have to be on my toes now with the tough competition I have next door."

"Ah, Lenore," said Andrew nodding his head. "Maybe I should have waited till I tried her pecan pie first before praising you on your lasagna?"

"Why, you, you…" she stuttered looking for the right word, but gave up, and chuckled instead.

"Nice come back."

"Actually, I'm usually much better, I'm just being polite," replied Gwyn in her defense and giving him a sweet smile.

"Would you like a piece of pie, perhaps?" he asked provokingly. "Or no, maybe just a coffee for you?"

"No perhaps! Of course I want a piece, I have to know what I am up against," she said watching him stand, "and coffee, too. Chop, chop!"

Andrew smiled at her as he picked up the dirty plates and turned for the kitchen. "Look who decided to join us," he said looking down at Magic.

Magic brushed against his leg, went under the dining room table, then jumped on the couch.

"I wonder where he was?" asked Gwyn.

"He probably found a comfy spot somewhere upstairs," replied Andrew.

Chapter Six

When the Mass ended Andrew and Gwyn waited for all the parishioners to say goodbye to Father Malcolm before approaching him.

"Good morning, Father," said Gwyn.

"Gwyn, it's lovely to see you again. How are your parents, sister, and brother?"

"They are all doing well, thank you," she replied.

"Let them know I was asking after them."

"I will."

Father Malcolm looked over at Andrew.

"Good morning, Father."

"Good morning, Andrew. How are you doing?"

"Doing as well as can be expected," he replied. "I've just started to go through my great-uncle's personal items."

"I'm sure at times, it will be very trying and stressful," said Father Malcolm, "but if you keep your heart and mind open to what his possessions meant to him, you will connect with him on a much higher level and find it will be very rewarding and satisfying."

"Thank you," replied Andrew, "I'll try."

"Trying is the only chance for success, where if you never try, you have already failed," suggested Father Malcolm. "You must forgive me, philosophy was one of my favorite subjects in college," he said smiling back and forth at them, before stopping at Andrew who looked preoccupied. "Andrew, is there something on your mind?"

"Actually Father, there is, I was wondering if my great-uncle had any personal items here, maybe ones that were locked up?"

Father Malcolm looked at him momentarily. "I believe all his items were boxed up and dropped off at his house."

"I thought so," said Andrew. "Thank you—"

"Hold on," said Father Malcolm. "There is a locked drawer in my desk that I couldn't find the key for, it was your great-uncle's, could that be it?"

"I'm not sure, can I have a look at it?"

"You can, but I can only spare you five minutes, I have to go do my rounds at the hospital," he explained.

They followed Father Malcolm through the church, passed the confessional boxes to the reception area, then went through the doors and turned into the second office on the right.

"Here it is," he said pointing at it.

Andrew went behind the desk, squatted, and looked at the lock. "I think one of the keys he gave me was for this," he said looking over at them. Then he noticed something peculiar. "Father Malcolm, did you try and open this drawer with a knife?"

"What?" asked Father Malcolm as he knelt down next to Andrew and examined the markings. "No, I didn't. These weren't here before. These are new," he said wondering who would have done such a thing as he stood up. "If I didn't find the key by the end of the week, I was going to call a locksmith."

"Well, if mine fits, and assuming it's my great-uncle's personal stuff inside, I'll remove the contents and you can keep the key."

"That would make it so much easier than calling someone," replied Father Malcolm flipping through his calendar. "I'm busy filling in at another parish Monday, Tuesday, and Wednesday. Why don't you come back Thursday morning at nine?"

"Okay, Father, we will see you then."

Father Malcolm followed them out of his office, then turned, and uncharacteristically locked his door.

Once outside, Gwyn and Andrew walked down Church Street before taking a left onto Liberty.

"This is downtown," said Gwyn as she stopped and started pointing. "Down there are several bars, pubs, and restaurants. There's the ice cream parlor, and right across the street is our local diner. The movie theatre is just over there, and a little further on, is the bowling alley and an arcade." She motioned across the street. "If you take Lake Road, it will lead you to 'Thornton Beach & Boardwalk' where they have summer touristy places. You know, restaurants, bars with patios, arcades, boutiques that sell swimwear and beach accessories, that sort of stuff. It's extremely popular, would you like to see it?"

"I'd love to," said Andrew enthusiastically. "But only, if you let me buy you lunch?"

"It's a da...deal," she replied catching herself.

They crossed the street and walked for fifteen minutes before arriving at the boardwalk.

"Let's go in here."

"Daisy's Bar and Patio," said Andrew reading the sign.

They sat on the deck, overlooking Skaneateles Lake, and ordered a couple of beers.

"You have a brother and sister?" asked Andrew.

"I do. I was going to tell you about them when I first met you, but with my bombardment of personal questions, I decided to save it for another day."

"Let me guess, you asked Father Malcolm to mention them in front of me?"

Gwyn laughed. "No, but now that you mention it, it wouldn't have been a bad idea," she said glancing guiltily away.

"Don't ever play cards Gwyn, you have the worst poker face."

"Is it that noticeable?"

"It is," he replied with a pleasant smile.

"Okay, every week after Mass he asks me about them," she clarified, "and let's say today, he didn't let me down."

Andrew shook his head dubiously.

"What?" she asked innocently, as they watched the waitress drop off their drinks.

"Tell me about your sister and brother."

"My sister is a lot like me and couldn't wait to get out of the city. She's a couple of years older, married, with two children, and lives in a town similar to Thornton, called Charlotte, which is also where her husband was born and raised. So after they finished college, they had no problem moving there," she explained. "Charlotte is on the other side of the lake, but just a little south of where we are situated. Do you know it?"

"I do," confirmed Andrew. "They're nice and close."

"I could actually sail a boat across and visit her," she said with a giggle, "if only I had a boat to sail!"

"Maybe one day you will," he replied with a smile. "Didn't I read somewhere that they're doing a big development along the waterfront to enhance tourism."

"They are. My sister works for the new developer selling residential properties, like houses, cottages, and lakefront apartments. She also leases commercial buildings and units for stores, bars, and boutiques that are going to be built along the waterfront and on the boardwalk. Her husband also works for them, he's a civil engineer."

"That's exciting."

"It is. They're both really happy, and I'm happy for them too," she said as she thought of them momentarily. "Now, my younger brother on the other hand, is the total opposite of us. He loves his condo, his office, and a vacation to him is a five-star all-inclusive resort," she said with a chuckle. "But he's really a great guy and would give you the shirt off his back." Gwyn stopped and glanced at Andrew briefly. "They would both like you," she said candidly before picking up her drink and taking a sip. "You've never mentioned siblings, so I'm guessing you have none?"

"If I did, I would have mentioned it to Father Malcolm, so he could ask me how they are doing in front of you," ribbed Andrew.

Gwyn laughed. "You're never going to let that one go, are you?"

"Uh-uh, that's gold," he said taking a swig of his beer. He liked how open and honest she was, and how easy it was to talk to her, and it felt good.

"Gwyn!" shouted a voice coming across the patio.

"Daisy!" she yelled back and stood up to embrace her dear friend.

"How've you been girlfriend?"

"I've been good, keeping busy."

"I heard you moved back into your parent's place, what took you so long to come and see me?" she asked, then noticed Andrew. "Well, there's my answer," she said looking back at her friend. "Gwyn, you've hit the jackpot!"

"He's not my boyfriend, this is my neighbor, and friend Andrew," clarified Gwyn.

Daisy gave her a look of disbelief. "If you say so," she said with a wink, "but your secret is safe with me."

"You haven't changed a bit, always stirring up trouble."

"It's only trouble, if you don't want them around," said Daisy gesturing to Andrew with her shoulder before turning to him. "Sorry Andrew, I'm Daisy."

"Please to meet you."

"You too," replied Daisy before looking back to Gwyn. "So, what ever happened to that other guy you were seeing for a while?" asked Daisy straight faced.

Gwyn gave her a stunned look. "We broke up some time ago."

"Oh, sorry to hear that," she said with an exaggerated sad face. "Listen, I have to get back to running the place, but don't either of you be a stranger," she said glancing at Gwyn, then looking at Andrew. "Thursday is 'Ladies Night,' just saying."

"Will you stop? He's not interested in…" Gwyn caught herself. "I mean…"

Daisy laughed at her friend's gawkiness as she walked away. "Later guys."

Gwyn wanted to jump off the deck and hide under it.

"Ex-boyfriend?" needled Andrew. "Was that another set up?"

"That was an unexpected one for me, she probably thought I wanted her to ask me about my ex in front of you, you know, just to get it out there in the open."

"Do you want to talk about him?" asked Andrew trying not to laugh.

"Sure, it was a while back, we met in—"

"Just like that," said Andrew shaking his head and chuckling.

"I probably should've been a little less eager to tell you," she admitted, realizing her blunder.

"A little less may have been better, I may have actually believed it wasn't a set up."

"I told you; it wasn't a set up, it was—"

"I'm messing with you," he said grinning. "Go on, tell me."

"All right, and because you're being such a good sport about this, I'll give you the abbreviated version," said Gwyn with a happy smile. "Several years ago, we met, dated, and fell in love. He didn't want to move out here, ever, or even visit. To me, 'ever' is a very, very long time, and I didn't want to spend the rest of my life trying to convince him to change his mind. So, I broke up with him."

"Wow! That is an abbreviated version," conceded Andrew.

"Do you want the long one?" she asked ominously.

"No, no, I'm good," he said sitting way back in his chair and waving his hands.

"Oh, please stop!" she said giggling and sipping her beer. She knew she was falling for him.

"So after you split up, a few years later you moved back here?"

"Pretty much," she confirmed. "How about you, do you have any special somebody?"

"I see you're very shy?"

Gwyn laughed. "I'm sorry, I can't help it, I just like directness."

"I can tell, and I must admit, it's one of the many qualities I find very attractive about you."

Did he just say that? "I know, it's one of my many, many, fine qualities," she replied. Oh no, you idiot, why did you say that? Now you sound full of yourself. You should have just said thank you.

Andrew sensed her uncomfortableness and decided to have some fun. "Humble, too," he said sardonically and let his response hang in the air.

"I'm not conceited at all, you've got me all wrong, and I was just joking," she said defensively. "I was just a little surprised by your comment, and I replied vainly to hide my insecurity," she explained, and slowly made eye contact with him, then quickly realized something. "Why, you little fucker!" she whispered. "You knew that I wasn't like that, you just wanted to see me sit here and squirm!"

Andrew couldn't contain himself and broke out into a loud laughter.

"You are going to pay for that mister!" said Gwyn squeezing his hand. She tried to pull it back, but he held on to it tenderly for several moments before letting it go. She shyly smiled.

"I'm sorry, I couldn't resist, I saw an opportunity and I took it."

"Yes, at my expense," she said pretending to pout.

"Well, if it's any consolation, I meant what I said, and you're right, you do have many, many fine qualities."

"Thank you," she replied sincerely, and she knew right then and there, she had fallen for him.

"To get back to my many, many, many, girlfriends," he said leaning back in his chair. "Were do I begin?"

"Oh boy!" said Gwyn shaking her head. "At least let me get another drink before you start your saga."

They ordered two more and waited for the waitress to drop them off.

"Okay, lover boy, let's hear it!"

"Actually, I've only had a few over the past several years. My most recent girlfriend and I broke up four months ago, and we only dated for about six. And the girls I dated after her, were noticeably short term," he said glancing at her nervously. "Mostly, because of me."

Gwyn liked his honesty. "You're afraid to commit, huh?"

Andrew anxiously looked at her. "I guess."

"With what happened to you at the beginning of the year, that's understandable."

"I think that has a lot to do with it, and as much as I say I love the city, I think it reminds me of them too much, and not in a good way." Andrew thought for a moment. "But since being here, even with my great-uncle's passing, I don't feel the same way, and I'm not really sure why."

Gwyn studied him for a moment and thought about what he had just said. "I believe it's because your great-uncle lived an exceptionally long and fulfilling life, and you were a big part of his, and him, yours, and you were here when he quietly passed away in his sleep. Unfortunately, with your parents, you were denied all that," she said with a sorrowful look, and grabbed his hand.

Andrew squeezed it gently; he knew he was falling for her. "Thank you, that was well said. I guess we're both running away from something."

"Or maybe, we're both running towards the same thing," suggested Gwyn with a smile.

"Yeah, maybe we are," he replied, smiling back.

They gazed at each other fleetingly, took a sip of their drinks, then looked out at the lake.

Gwyn quickly turned to him. "Oh! What do you think is in that drawer?" she asked animatedly.

"I have no idea," he replied shaking his head. "Since I was given those keys, I've been wondering what my great-uncle could possibly have, that he would only want me to see."

Chapter Seven

On Tuesday evening, Andrew returned from the city, and pulled into his driveway. He removed a box from the back seat, walked up the steps to his porch, and sitting there was Magic.

"Hey, how are you doing boy? Are you waiting for me?" he asked. "Just let me put this in the den and I'll be right back." Andrew went inside, put the box on the desk, and when he came out Magic was gone. On the way to the car, out of the corner of his eye, he thought he saw Magic dashing across the street. He grabbed the last box, and was walking onto the porch, when Magic slowly came out from underneath the swing. "There you are! I thought you had taken off for a nighttime journey."

"You know they lock people up who have conversations with animals," joked Gwyn.

"Look Magic, my very own personal stalker," he replied with an impish smile.

"You wish."

"Well, I couldn't have asked for a prettier one," he said making her blush. "You have no comeback for that one, huh?"

"None needed when the truth is told," she said tilting her head sweetly and giving him a delightful smile.

"Oh boy, here we go!" he replied, shaking his head. "Do you want to grab the door after you've finished being adorable?"

"But I'm always adorable," she said opening it and following him to the den. "What's in the boxes?"

"It's just my writing stuff."

"You're going to start to write?" she asked excitedly as she sat on his desk.

"Probably," he replied.

"When?"

"Next week."

"Do you have a story in mind?"

"No."

"Setting?"

"I do."

"Where?"

"Thornton."

"You're going to write a story about here?" she asked doubtfully.

"I am," he replied. "What's with the face?"

"We have no murders here, in fact, we don't even have any crimes!"

"It's fictional…I'll make it up."

"Oh yeah, right," she said contemplating briefly. "Do you have any thoughts on characters? Maybe somebody who lives in this town?"

"Actually…I have two in mind."

"Two!" she repeated ecstatically. "Who?"

Andrew leaned over and whispered. "Can you keep a secret?"

"Yes," she whispered back leaning close to him.

Andrew amusingly looked side to side, then directly at her, and said in a low voice, "one character is a very talkative obnoxious witch, who asks a lot of questions, and lives right next door; the other, is Lenore."

As she watched him leave, it took a moment for it to register. "Why you little," she said quickly following him into the kitchen, "fucker! I—"

"Can now, definitely add profanity to your character," he declared as she slowly approached him.

"I ought to—"

"You ought to, what?" he asked pulling her close to him and kissing her softly on the lips.

Gwyn responded by gently kissing him back.

Edwin tied the belt around his arm, inserted the needle into his pulsating vein, and slowly pressed down. Once emptied, he quickly removed the needle, undid the belt, and placed them on the table, then waited for the heroin to kick in. Suddenly, he felt something breathing and slowly looked up at the black cat lying on top of the couch next to him.

"Hey, Magic," he mumbled. "What are you doing here?"

Magic purred.

"Do you want a hit little dude?"

Magic jumped down onto the couch, then onto the coffee table, and motioned with its paw at the heroin.

"Really?" asked Edwin sitting up.

The black cat lay down, looked at him, and waited.

"I must be pretty messed up," said Edwin, reaching out to pat his hallucination, but ending up stroking Magic.

Magic meowed loudly.

"Okay, kitty, I'll fix you up," said Edwin heating up the heroin in a spoon, placing the tip of the needle into it, and sucking it up. "We're all good to go, little dude. Now all you need to do is put your arm like this," explained Edwin, laying his forearm down on the table, with his veins showing.

Magic lay on his side and put his front right leg over Edwin's exposed forearm.

"I can't see any of your veins, so I'm just going to jab it in quick and hard, so keep still," instructed Edwin, lifting the needle over his head in his right hand and placing his thumb over the top of the plunger. "Okay, on three...one, two, three." As Edwin swiftly brought the syringe down, Magic quickly moved out of the way, causing Edwin to stab the needle deep into his own vein.

Magic slowly put his right paw on Edwin's forearm, then put his left paw on Edwin's thumb, and gently pushed down on the plunger, releasing the heroin.

By the time Edwin realized what was going on, it was too late. He fell to the floor, and within minutes, was dead.

The black cat stared down into Edwin's vacant eyes, then left.

"Would you like some more wine?" asked Andrew standing.

"Yes, please," she replied handing him her glass.

Something caught Andrew's eye. He went to the end of the porch and looked in the direction of Lenore's house and spotted Magic crossing the street. "There's Magic, I thought I saw him," he said pointing, as Gwyn joined him.

"Oh yeah," she said noticing him too. "I guess he went on a little trip."

"Is that him?" questioned Andrew as he watched Magic cross Lenore's front lawn, go up toward the side of the neighbor's house, and disappear.

"It looked like him," said Gwyn turning, looking at Andrew, and lifting up her empty glass. "Do you want me to get the wine?"

"No, I got it," he replied.

Gwyn moved close to him and gently kissed him on the lips. "Don't be long."

"I won't."

Suddenly, Magic appeared from under the swing.

"Here he is," said Gwyn noticing him first, "it must have been him!" She crouched down, caressed him briefly, then picked him up and placed him in his basket. "This is yours, and it has a soft fancy cushion for you to lie on, do you like it?"

Magic curled up and purred softly as she continued to stroke him.

Andrew glanced over at the neighbor's house, then back at Magic. "I guess you're right."

Chapter Eight

Early the following morning there was a knock on the door; Andrew left the kitchen and opened it.

"Good morning, sorry to bother you, my name is Deputy Sheriff Williams. I was wondering if I could have a moment of your time?"

The tone of the deputy sheriff's question sounded as if they knew one another. Although Andrew couldn't remember meeting him, he did look vaguely familiar. "Have we met before?"

"My apologies. We did at your great-uncle's funeral, I was in civilian clothes, and was one of the pallbearers."

"Montgomery, Montgomery Williams," recalled Andrew.

"Yes, sir. Again, my condolences for your loss."

"Thank you," replied Andrew. "Would you like to come in Deputy Sheriff Williams? I just made a fresh pot of coffee."

"I would appreciate that, and please, call me Monty," he said following Andrew into the kitchen.

"Okay, Monty, how do you take it?"

"Black is fine," he answered removing his hat, placing it on the table, and taking a seat.

Andrew passed Monty his coffee and sat opposite him.

"First, although I am in uniform, I want you to know that this is strictly off the record."

"All right," agreed Andrew curiously.

"I understand in the city, you teach criminology at Syracuse University, and also down in Cortland, and you're a professor?

"That's right."

"I also heard from my associates there, that you have helped them out on several high-level cases, with great success."

Andrew shifted uneasily in his chair. "Well, I really can't discuss—"

"Off the record," reiterated Monty.

"Unofficially," said Andrew cautiously, "I have."

"The reason I'm here, is that I need your help," said Monty forthright.

"Help with what?" asked Andrew looking at him inquisitively. "From what I've heard, this town has no homicides."

"That's true," he said, "but there is something that has me mystified, and before I write it off as being my imagination, I would like a second opinion. A professional opinion."

Andrew's interest was now piqued. "What do you want me to do?"

"If you have some time this morning, I would like you to come to a crime scene with me?"

"You mean a homicide crime scene?"

"Not exactly," said Monty. "Right now, it's being deemed as an accident or a suicide."

Andrew looked at him deep in thought. "Okay, give me ten minutes."

"Thank you," he said standing and putting on his hat. "I'll wait for you in the cruiser."

Andrew watched the deputy sheriff leave, then quickly glanced upstairs, he hoped she was still asleep, but no such luck.

"Well, well, well, Mr. Andrew Blake, there is more to you than meets the eye," said Gwyn mischievously sitting up on the bed.

"What did you hear?"

"I heard from, 'Good morning, sorry to bother you,' right up to, 'I'll wait for you in my cruiser.'"

He shook his head disapprovingly, and tried to act upset with her, but couldn't. "Promise me you won't say a word about this to anyone?"

She realized he was anxious about her knowing. "I promise, I won't…but, on one condition."

"Please, no conditions, this isn't a game."

"I never said it was," she retorted. "I thought we had an open relationship and could talk about anything."

"We do, and I'm sorry, I didn't mean it like that," he said putting his arms around her and kissing her cheek. "Please, forgive me, I'm just a little anxious."

She looked at him. "I know you are," she said in a kind voice, and softly caressed his cheek. "Besides, I could never be upset with you."

Andrew took her hand and gently kissed it. "Now, what's your condition?"

"That you tell me everything, no secrets?"

Andrew smiled at her. He thought back to when he was helping the city detectives, at that time he had no one to confide in, and how often he wished he had someone. And here she was, offering it all to him, on one simple condition.

"I think that's fair, don't you," she asked wondering what he was thinking about.

"It's more than fair," he replied.

"Good," she said happy with herself and laying on the bed. "Oh, you can go now."

"What am I going to do with you?"

"When you come home, the same as last night," she suggested with a wink.

"Deal," he said kissing her tenderly on the lips.

She responded by putting her arms around him, pulling him down on top of her, and kissing him passionately, before letting him go, and watching him get changed.

"I made a fresh pot of coffee," he said walking to the door and opening it, "and if I'm going to be a while, I'll text you."

"Okay," she said kneeling on the bed and blowing him a kiss. She then listened to him go down the stairs and outside, before running to the window, and watching him jump into the cruiser.

"The victim is a male, in his mid-thirties, and a well-known drug dealer," explained Monty. "He gave a group of teenagers some bad drugs a few years back, one of them overdosed, and luckily for him the boy fully recovered. He ended up giving state's evidence and never did time. A few months later, there were reports that several teenagers died in the city from the same drug, we could never pin it on him, but we're pretty certain it was."

"How was he found?"

"I would prefer you to see it firsthand," replied Monty, pulling up to the crime scene, then looking over at him. "What I really need to know, is whether this was an accident or a suicide, or made to look like either, to cover up a murder."

Monty asked Andrew to wait, then went ahead and cleared everyone out of the house, before escorting him in. Inside, they put on latex gloves, then walked over to the victim.

Andrew carefully examined the body. "He shot himself up twice. The first, was done slowly, carefully, meticulously, and the second, was a reckless, jab to the arm."

"That's our assessment, too," confirmed Monty. "His prints are on the needle, and they are the only ones here, with the exception of the cat's pawprints and hair."

Andrew looked at the white pawprints on the table. "What did the cat step in?"

"It's talcum powder. I'm guessing the victim didn't like to have sweaty hands and must have accidentally knocked the container over. There's a layer of it on the couch next to where the deceased was sitting," said Monty pointing. "It looks like the cat jumped from the top of the couch, onto the seat cushion, got the powder on its paws, and then jumped onto the table."

Andrew looked at the pawprints on the couch. "Does he own a cat?"

"Not that we are aware of, and he didn't have cat food or a litter box, but there are strays around here that people feed, and it could have been just that. The living room window was slightly open, so it probably came in through there."

"A cat's not going to inject anyone," said Andrew standing up.

"So, is it an accident or a suicide?"

"Well, looking at the tracks on his arms, he was very careful about shooting up. But the one that killed him, I would definitely say is out of character…maybe he was having a bad trip or hallucinations."

"There was no suicide note and speaking with his friends they said he was acting normal, well, he was acting like his usual self," clarified Monty.

"I think we can conclude it's not a murder. It's your call as to whether you want to report it as an accident or suicide," said Andrew looking down at the body then Monty. "Does he have any family?"

"Parents and a younger sister, and from what I understand, his parents were putting money together to get him set up in a rehab."

They left the crime scene, got into the cruiser, and drove in silence for a while.

"Can I ask you something that may sound odd?"

"Sure," replied Andrew.

"Did your great-uncle ever give you something, like a document, that you considered out of the ordinary?"

"I went through his stuff at the house, and whatever was dropped off by the church, but nothing stuck out. Most of it was photos, cards, and thank you notes from the parishioners, along with the ones that I had sent him over the years," he said looking over at Monty. "With the exception of the ones I had given him, I was going to throw the rest out, do you want them?"

"No, if you didn't notice anything out of the ordinary, neither would we," replied Monty pulling into Andrew's driveway. "Thanks again."

"Anytime," replied Andrew getting out, closing the door, and walking away before stopping and coming back.

Monty put down the passenger window.

"Out of idle curiosity, is this the first strange incident you've had?"

Monty hesitated, looked around nervously then back at Andrew, and shook his head no.

Andrew thought for a moment, said "goodbye," and left.

Monty watched Andrew and thought about going after him, to query him as to why he asked that question, but didn't see the point at this time and decided to drive away instead.

"Tell me, tell me!" said Gwyn sitting up on the bed and drinking her coffee.

Andrew told her.

"That's Edwin, I know him, that's so sad."

"He had a lot of tracks up and down both of his arms."

"His poor parents and sister, they must be devastated," she said glumly. "Are they going to rule it an accident or a suicide?"

"I didn't ask Monty, but I'm guessing for the sake of his family, he will say it was an accidental overdose."

"I really hope so," stated Gwyn. "Is that all Monty wanted you for?"

"Yep," replied Andrew.

She leaned over and kissed him. "Thank you for sharing that with me."

"I'm glad I have you to share it with," said Andrew sincerely, and gently caressed her hair. "Are you hungry?"

"I'm starving!"

"Do you want me to make us some breakfast?"

"No, let's make it together," she said, grabbing his hand and leading him downstairs to the kitchen.

Chapter Nine

Gwyn and Andrew arrived at the church at nine and were greeted in the reception area by Lenore.

"I see you have an appointment with Father Malcolm," she said looking over at the calendar. "He will be a few minutes late, he had to make a stop at the hospital on the way here."

"That's all right," said Andrew, "we're in no rush."

"What's the appointment about?" asked Lenore making small talk.

"We're getting married," joked Gwyn.

"Oh, stop it!" said Lenore laughing.

"It's regarding my great-uncle," revealed Andrew. "I told Father Malcolm that I was going through some of his personal items, and he is going to give me some spiritual advice and guidance."

"And some philosophical advice, too," kidded Gwyn.

"He loves his philosophy; he has books and books on the subject."

"Sorry I'm late," said Father Malcolm walking in.

They followed the priest, waited for him to unlock his door, and went inside. Andrew tried the first key, it didn't work, then the second, and the drawer unlocked. Andrew pulled it open, inside was a satchel, and he lifted it out.

"There's a sticky note on it," said Gwyn pulling it off. "It says, 'Property of Andrew Blake.'"

Andrew looked at the note then at Father Malcolm. "Do you need me to open this in front of you?"

"No," he replied. "Your great-uncle left that for you, and I doubt there is anything of value for the church inside. Please, take it and open it in the privacy of your home."

Andrew removed the key and gave it to the priest. "Thank you, Father," he said, then headed for the door with Gwyn, and was about to open it.

"If you're great-uncle left that just for you, he meant for it not to be shared lightly, be careful who you show it to," warned Father Malcolm.

Andrew and Gwyn looked at one another then left. Lenore was on the phone, so they just waved bye to her, and walked outside.

Once on the street, Gwyn looked at him. "What was that all about? It sounded very foreboding."

"I'm not sure," said Andrew shaking his head, "but I get the feeling Father Malcolm knows something."

They went into the diner, sat in a booth, and ordered breakfast.

"When are you going to open it?" asked Gwyn.

"When we get home."

"We," she repeated with a happy grin, then noticed the deputy sheriff walking in. "It's Monty, he's looking for someone."

Monty spotted Gwyn, then Andrew, and walked over to them. "Mind if I join you for a quick coffee?"

"Not at all," said Gwyn.

"Please, sit and join us," offered Andrew.

Monty grabbed a chair and sat.

"How did you know we were here?"

"I was heading to your place and seen you two in my rearview mirror crossing over to the diner, so I turned around."

"Something's on your mind?" asked Andrew.

"Actually, there is," he said quietly and looked at Andrew. "Can we talk in private?"

"Is it to do with my question from yesterday?"

"It is," replied Monty, "it's been on my mind since..." He stopped and quickly glanced over at Gwyn.

"Do you want me to go and sit at the counter?" she asked.

Before Monty could answer, Andrew did. "No, that won't be necessary," he said to Gwyn and looked over at Monty. "When we talked at my place, Gwyn was upstairs, and heard us. And when I got back, I told her about Edwin. She's promised me, she wouldn't tell a soul, and I believe her."

"I've known Gwyn for most of her life, and I've never heard her lie once, her word is good with me, too," he said giving her a smile before looking back at Andrew. "This conversation is still unofficial, of course."

"Of course," replied Andrew.

Feeling more at ease, Monty spoke freely. "'Out of idle curiosity, is this, the first strange incident you've had?'" said Monty quoting Andrew. "Now, I can't say I know you all that well, but I don't believe you have idle curiosity."

"Oh, he doesn't!" confirmed Gwyn.

They both looked at Andrew.

"You asked me yesterday if Edwin's death was an accident, a suicide, or a murder. In any crime scene, after you review all the facts, you eventually come up with your decision. Now, if you remove those same facts, whatever you are left with, however improbable, is the only alternative to that decision."

"And what 'is the only alternative to that decision,' for Edwin's death?" asked Gwyn.

"The cat."

"The cat!" said Monty with a surprised look.

"I know," said Andrew running his fingers through his hair. "Hearing me say it worries me too."

"You said the cat couldn't have injected him."

"I know, I know," repeated Andrew agitatedly.

"Just explain to us what you mean," suggested Gwyn.

"I'll try," he said, gathering his thoughts. "Edwin was a heroin addict, who was careful and vigilant, and only injected set doses. Then all of a sudden, he just stabs himself deep into his arm and OD's, it just doesn't add up...Now bear with me, let's take away all the facts for it being considered an accident or a suicide: the heroin, the needle, his body, his finger prints, and even the talcum powder…All that we are left with at the scene, are the cat's pawprints and hair."

Monty sat back in his chair and looked over at Gwyn, before looking back at Andrew. "Do you know how crazy this sounds?"

"I know, I know," replied Andrew struggling with it too.

The waitress brought their breakfasts, refilled their coffees, and left.

In the awkward silence, Andrew thought about what he had said. Suddenly, something came back to him, that had made him think about the cat in the first place. "How many incidents?"

"What?" asked Monty, putting his coffee down.

"How many strange incidents so far?"

Monty whispered. "Over these last two weeks, including yesterday, three."

"Three!" said Gwyn in a quiet voice. "How many in total?"

"Seven in the last eight months."

Gwyn looked on in amazement.

"There's a simple way of clearing this up," said Andrew.

"I'm listening," replied Monty.

"Do you still have photos, fingerprints, and hair samples from the two previous victim's crime scenes?"

"We do."

"Check and see if there was a cat present. If not, then these were all unfortunate accidents. If there is, then try cross-referencing them, and see if you find any matches."

"Even if a cat was there, all we are left with, is just a cat," said Monty simplifying it.

"True, but if there is no cat present at either of them, then you could list them all as accidents, and put all this behind you," he replied. "You wanted my professional opinion, so let's gather all the facts, and I'll make one."

"All right," said Monty, "I will put the guys in the lab to work and see what they come up with."

Andrew thought momentarily. "Where's Edwin's body?"

"At the morgue," replied Monty. "They're moving him to the funeral home this afternoon."

"Send one of your guys over there as soon as you can."

"Why? What for?"

"Have them check for prints on Edwin's forearm, from the last needle insertion to his wrist, and also around the fingernail area of his right thumb," requested Andrew.

"Why?" asked Monty.

"I just want to eliminate all possible scenarios," replied Andrew, "and I'm sure you do, too."

"I'll go back to the station and send someone over there straight away," said Monty quickly finishing his coffee and saying goodbye.

Andrew and Gwyn ate their breakfast in silence. He was having a difficult time with what he had said about the cat, but something didn't feel right. She wanted to say something to comfort him, without sounding condescending, but decided to say nothing.

When they left the diner, Andrew put his arm around her. "You know, when Monty comes back telling us that there was no cat at the other two crime scenes, we can both laugh at this over a few glasses of wine."

Gwyn stopped and looked at him.

"What's wrong? What's the matter?"

"You're scaring me."

"What? Why?"

"Because I know, that you know, they will find traces of a cat at the other two crime scenes, and you will be right...and that you know, they will also find traces of a cat's pawprint on Edwin's forearm and thumb...and that scares me, actually it terrifies me," she said staring at him. "Am I right? If I'm not, please, tell me I'm wrong?"

He looked at the ground, to the side, anywhere but in her eyes.

"Andrew, look at me. Look at me!" she pleaded.

Andrew did.

"Are they going to find traces of a cat at the other two crime scenes?"

"No," he replied slowly, "they're going to find it at all seven."

"What! What does that mean?" she asked, frightened.

"I don't know, and I won't know for sure, until they share all the information they have with me."

Gwyn nervously nodded her head up and down, and asked, "I'm I also right to think that they will find a cat's pawprint on Edwin's forearm and thumb?"

"Yes, from the talcum powder."

"Why would you think a cat's pawprint would be on his forearm and thumb? Why?" she asked frantically.

"You're going to think it sounds crazy," replied Andrew calmly.

"Oh yes, and everything you have told me so far, has sounded so normal," she said cynically. "I can see why you would be concerned for my sanity now."

"Gwyn, are you okay?" he asked tenderly squeezing her arm.

"No, I'm not!" she replied anxiously. "Just tell me!"

Andrew took a deep breath. "I think the cat was coaxing or taunting Edwin. Then Edwin went to inject the cat, missed, and mistakenly stabbed the needle deep into his arm. Then I think the cat…" Andrew stopped.

"Think the cat, what? What?" asked Gwyn impatiently waiting for him to continue.

"I think the cat put its right paw on Edwin's forearm, balanced itself, and placed its left paw on Edwin's thumb, pushed down, and released the heroin into his vein."

"Why would you think that, hmm? Why?" she asked hysterically.

"If Edwin had realized he had mistakenly stabbed his arm, instead of the cat's leg, I don't think he would have pressed down, and inserted himself with a second lethal dose of heroin. He would have known the outcome, and instead, safely removed the needle."

"You know Andrew, this is fucking creeping me out!" she said losing it.

"I know," he said gently embracing her.

Gwyn held him for as long as she needed, then pulled away, and wiped her eyes. "I'm sorry, I'm sorry I freaked out."

"It's okay," he said comforting her. "I've done that a few times myself, in the city, when I was helping them out."

"You have?"

Andrew nodded. "Sometimes it's difficult to wrap your head around things that are surreal," he confessed. "You witnessed me in the diner, I was this close to losing it."

"Yeah, you were," she said laughing a little.

"I'm just jealous that I didn't get to freak out like you did, I'm sure you feel a hell of a lot better now."

"You know, I do," she admitted with a smile, then looked into his eyes. "I know I gave you a condition to tell me everything, and you have. You said this wasn't a game, and you were right, it isn't. I just want you to know that if I can help you in any way I can, I will, and that you have my support, no matter what."

"I know I do," he said giving her a soft kiss on the lips.

She grabbed him and kissed him back intensely. "Now, let's go open that satchel!"

Chapter Ten

Andrew placed the satchel on the kitchen table, unlocked it, and looked inside. He pulled out a folder and a USB flash drive. He placed them down, opened the folder, and removed the thicker of the two documents, and leafed through it as Gwyn looked on.

"This is a spreadsheet with a list of names, and next to each of them, are all the sins they have committed; below that, a description of the person; under that, what they are guilty of; and then their sentence." He gave Gwyn a perplexed glance then returned to the document. "Look at this one," he said pointing. "Name: Davis Todd; Sins: Adulterer, liar, womanizer; Description: Known around town, and in the city, as a player, his friends nickname for him is 'Zipper' because his pants zipper is always down; Guilty of: Adultery; Sentence: None."

"I know him, he lives on the other side of town," said Gwyn looking at Andrew, then at the document. "Why are some highlighted in blue?"

Andrew picked the most recent. "Name: Jean Laurence; Sins: Murder, alcoholic; Description: Drunk who got off with killing a ten-year-old girl while under the influence; Guilty of: Murder; Sentence: Death." Andrew sat down and looked at Gwyn. "Do you know her too?"

"I do," she replied. "She lives just on the outskirts of town. One afternoon, a couple of months ago, she was drunk, lost control of her car, went up on the sidewalk, and crushed a young girl, who was riding her bike, against the wall. The girl was Betty-Jo, and she died instantly. Jean was charged with murder but got off on a technicality and was released."

"Is Jean Laurence dead?"

"No, I saw her the other day, she was very drunk, actually, she's rarely sober," replied Gwyn, reaching over, picking up the one-page document, and reviewing it. "Oh my God!" she said standing up horrified.

"What?" asked Andrew joining her.

"Look at number seven."

Andrew read the name aloud, "Edwin Edwards." He quickly flipped through the spreadsheet and found his name highlighted in blue. "Name: Edwin Edwards; Sins: Murder and attempted murder; Description: Drug dealer who ruins people's lives, gave bad drugs to teenagers, almost killed one of them in town, gave state's evidence and was released, killed three in the city, never charged; Guilty of: Murder, attempted murder; Sentence: Death." Andrew looked at her. "I'm going to read the highlighted names and you check to see if they are on the list." After he finished, he glanced over.

"All eight are on here," confirmed Gwyn. "The most recent name is at the bottom, that's Jean Laurence's, she's number eight."

Andrew flipped through his document to the back. "The last entry was six weeks ago," he said before going to the front, "and the first entry, is over eleven months ago. There are approximately ten names per page and over twenty pages, yet only eight are highlighted, and they're all sentenced to death."

Gwyn took the document from him and examined it. "Those eight had the most severe sins, because what they did - DUI, drug dealing, domestic violence, prostitution, and so on - either brought death or harm to individuals or were deemed extremely immoral. While the other sins on the spreadsheet are extremely low key, well, if you consider, adultery, stealing, and lying as low key in comparison."

"I wonder what these signify?" asked Andrew pointing over Gwyn's shoulder. "The 'Sins' heading has the word, 'box,' in brackets; while the 'Description' heading has the word, 'mouth.'

"I don't know," she replied, "they must mean something, otherwise, why have them." She started turning the pages and noticed something else. "For some names, under the 'Sins' heading, it's blank, meaning there's no information; and for other names, under the 'Description' heading, that's blank."

"This has me baffled," said Andrew apprehensively.

"What worries me more," asked Gwyn slowly, "is how your great-uncle came across these documents? They're obviously not his."

"I don't know," replied Andrew, "but that's a good question."

Gwyn reached for the flash drive. "Maybe this can help us?" She followed Andrew into the den, where he turned on his laptop, while she put the drive into the USB port.

"Two files: one is called 'Sentence,' and the other, 'Evidence.' He clicked on 'Sentence,' and it brought up the one-page list of names, then 'Evidence,' which brought up the spreadsheet. He closed them both, then looked up at Gwyn.

"Open 'Sentence' again and click on 'File'… there, under Properties. 'Title: Sentence; Status: Active; Subject: To Death; Author: Black Magic…Now, close that one down, and do the same with 'Evidence.'" She waited for him, then read them. "Title: Evidence; Status: Closed; Subject: Judge, Jury, Sentence, and Executioner; Author: Black Magic." Gwyn moved away from the screen, sat on his desk, and faced him. "What the…?"

"You took the words right out of my mouth," said Andrew leaning back in his chair. "Why is the 'Evidence' file's status closed?"

As Gwyn looked at him, she thought out loud. "All the names are people from this town…maybe the individual has collected all the information they need, or can, on the townspeople."

"Yes, and if there's no new information to add, it just becomes repetitive." Andrew left, went to the kitchen, and brought everything back. "Look here," he said pointing to a name in the spreadsheet, "June Watkins, she shows up almost every fourth Saturday, and has the exact same entry. Sins: Losing her temper, cheating at cards; Description: Kind, friendly, thoughtful; Guilty Of: Cheating; Sentence: Heaven."

"I thought the cat-thing was fucked up," said Gwyn, "this is truly fucked up!"

Andrew looked up at her. "For someone who teaches elementary children, you have quite the potty-mouth."

"It's not every day, you come across this shit!" she said poking fun at him.

"True," he said with a snicker, then went serious again. "First things first, let's take care of the satchel. Do you have any good cookie recipes?"

"I have a chocolate chip one."

"Do you know the ingredients and instructions?"

"I do."

"Okay, I need you to take a seat in front of my laptop, and type, 'Grandma's Secret Chocolate Chip Cookie Recipe,' as the heading, and under that type your grandma's ingredients and the instructions."

She gave him an odd look as she sat down.

"What?"

"Oh, nothing," she replied and started to type.

Andrew watched her till she was done, then printed it out. He got a tissue, picked up the printed recipe and placed it in the folder, put the folder inside the satchel and locked it up. Then he took the key, and put it in his desk drawer, before leaning the satchel against a filing cabinet with its lock facing inward."

"What are you doing?"

"Someone tried to get this satchel from Father Malcolm's desk."

"You're referring to the knife scratches?"

"Yes," he replied. "Chances are they may come here looking for it. If they do, they can have it, or at least what's inside."

"You're clever," she said, "warped, but clever."

"I get it from you," he said tickling her.

Gwyn laughed and pushed him away.

"Now, what to do with these documents and flash drive?"

"Wait, you're not going to give them to the deputy sheriff?" asked Gwyn, surprised.

"Not just yet, in a couple of days."

"What about Jean Laurence, she's the last person alive on that list, and her life is in danger."

"I know, I'll take care of that," he said reassuringly. "Remember what Father Malcolm said, 'if you're great-uncle left that just for you, he meant for it not to be shared lightly, be careful who you show it to,' I think that's a good piece of advice."

Gwyn nodded in agreement. "I know where you can put them," she said taking the documents and flash drive from him and heading for the kitchen. She placed them in a Ziploc freezer bag, opened the fridge, pulled out a crisper drawer, and put the bag at the back behind the lettuce and tomatoes, then pushed the drawer in, and closed the fridge. "What?" she asked looking at his reaction.

"You say, I'm warped."

"Trust me. How often does a thief rummage through a refrigerator?"

"You have a valid point," he said with a grin. "I think you're catching on very quickly."

"I'm learning from the best," she said kissing him on the cheek.

He grabbed her hand and led her into the living room where they sat on the couch. "Now, what do we have so far…a cat that may, or may not, be involved." As he said that, Magic meowed from his basket. "He seems to believe one is." They both laughed. "We have two documents: one that was used to gather evidence, and the other is a list of people's names, who have been sentenced to death."

"I may be naïve," said Gwyn, "and I know a cat is capable of doing many wonderful things, but gathering information, and putting together a spreadsheet is quite a stretch."

"I know," concurred Andrew.

"So, if we take the cat out of the equation, what we are left with are the spreadsheet and a list of names, which means that a person, or people, are involved."

"Very impressive," said Andrew.

"Thank you," replied Gwyn, happy with her summation.

"But who?" asked Andrew. "The author is named, 'Black Magic,' but why? Is that their name, the group's name, or what they practice? And how does the cat fit in to all this?"

"A lot of questions," stated Gwyn. "Maybe we should wait till we hear back from Monty before we spend too much time trying to figure out how the cat fits in. What do you think?"

"I agree," said Andrew sitting back, contemplating, and concluding that there was not much more they could do at this time. "Do you fancy a walk into town?"

"I do."

Chapter Eleven

A couple of hours later they returned from their walk. Monty was waiting in his cruiser, got out, and met them on the sidewalk. "Do you mind if we talk inside?"

They sat around the kitchen table while the coffee brewed.

"Upon your request, we did some further analysis on the cat, and went through our crime scene photos and hair samples," he said slowly.

"And?" asked Gwyn impatiently.

"At Emma Cooke's crime scene, there was evidence of a cat being present in the bathroom. There were pawprints on the wet tiled floor and black hair on the toilet lid cover. She didn't own a cat."

Gwyn gasped.

"At Al Smith's, we found a partial pawprint in the pool of blood, and black cat hair on his clothing. Judging by the pawprint, it was speculated that the cat was on the victim's chest, jumped off, and its back-right paw landed in the blood. I say speculated, because we need to run some additional tests, but the lab technician gave me a ninety-nine percent probability that's what happened. The Smith's didn't own a cat either."

"So three out of three," said Gwyn.

"Not exactly," said Monty restlessly. "They went back to the remaining four victims, and also found evidence of a black cat being present."

Gwyn looked at Andrew who was quiet then back at Monty. "What about the forearm and right thumb?" asked Gwyn, wondering why she was taking the lead.

"The talcum powder left faint, partial pawprints on both the forearm and right thumb."

Andrew ran his fingers through his hair. Then stood up and poured three cups of coffee. Placed them on the table, along with cream and sugar, and sat down again. "Can you tell us the names of the victims and give us some background information on them?" he asked. "Unofficially, of course."

Monty went through all seven; from the most recent to the first. The names matched the list they had found in the satchel. Gwyn looked at Andrew waiting to see what he would say.

"Has there been a tragic death recently, where someone was killed?"

Monty looked at Andrew curiously. "There was an incident a couple of months ago involving a young girl, who was killed by a drunk driver, while riding her bike on the sidewalk. The woman was arrested, let off on a technicality, and was released."

"She's next," declared Andrew.

"How can you be so sure?"

"Most of these people that are dying, have been killed because of the heinous crimes they've committed, unless there is someone else in this town that has done something more atrocious than her, she's next."

The deputy sheriff silently looked over at Gwyn and back at Andrew.

"Can you offer her some kind of protection?" he asked.

"I will talk to her and put her under surveillance."

"Thank you," said Gwyn relieved.

"There is one more thing, before I go," said Monty standing up. "With the last two victims, Edwin Edwards and Emma Cooke, because they were considered homicide crime scenes, we had the whole house checked from top to bottom."

Andrew gave him a puzzled look. "Did you find anything?"

"A lot of black cat hair. It seems like the cat may have been living there for a while."

"Living there?" repeated Gwyn.

"Before I came over here, I spoke with Jane Smith, and asked her if she had a stray cat staying in their house. She said no, but she did have a cat that came to visit them every so often, only in the evenings. Jane said it was playful, liked attention, and was very fond of Al, and that it used to follow him around the house.”

“But Jane said it wasn’t a stray?” asked Gwyn, confused.

“It wasn’t, because Jane said she knew the cat well,” replied Monty. “She said the cat was Magic.”

“Magic!” said Gwyn shocked and looking over at Andrew. “How can that be?”

“She seemed quite certain,” replied Monty putting on his hat.

Andrew and Gwyn stood and walked him to the door.

“If you think of something, anything, let me know,” said Monty. “I’ll keep in touch. Thanks for the coffee and have a good night.”

They said goodnight and watched him walk down the path.

When Gwyn turned to talk to Andrew, he wasn’t there, and heard him in the kitchen. As she walked in that direction, he met her on the way, and handed her a beer.

“Come on, let’s go outside and talk.”

Gwyn and Magic followed and joined him on the patio swing.

“Something’s troubling you?”

“The deputy sheriff’s lying.”

“Lying? What? Why? How do you know?”

“He just said that the last two victims were homicide crime scenes. That morning in the kitchen, when he asked me for my help and professional opinion, I asked him what he wanted me to do. He said to come to a crime scene with him. I asked him, and I quote, ‘You mean a homicide crime scene?’ He replied, ‘not exactly, right now, it’s been deemed an accident or suicide.’”

“Now that you mention it, I remember overhearing that when I was upstairs in the bedroom. So, there would be no need for a top to bottom check?”

“No,” said Andrew stumped, “but he conducted one anyway.”

“Why?”

“That’s a good question Gwyn.”

Gwyn sipped her beer and stroked Magic. "What about Jane Smith saying Magic was visiting them?"

Andrew looked down at him. "I believe she had a cat in her house, but I don't think it was Magic."

"Supposing it isn't, is it the same stray cat visiting, and possibly staying with each of the victims? And if so, why?"

"That's two more good questions Gwyn," said Andrew taking a long swig. "I'm guessing the cat was stalking its victims, maybe looking for accessibility, bad habits, and calculating its murder."

"Really?" she asked doubtingly. "How could a cat behave that way, it's just not possible."

"I don't know," he replied. "I have a difficult time believing it myself, and I just said it."

"But Andrew, if what you are saying is true, the only way a cat could act that way would be if it were possessed," said Gwyn looking at him. "And if that was the case, that would mean that the person or people who created those documents, are using black magic to possess this stray black cat and commit murders."

"Gwyn, that's a good hypothesis, and one I would tend to agree with at this time."

"This continues to get more and more—"

"Fucked up by the minute," suggested Andrew.

"Yeah, by the minute," said Gwyn.

"I totally agree."

Chapter Twelve

"Thanks for coming with me to Edwin's funeral," said Gwyn as they pulled into the church parking lot.

"No problem," replied Andrew.

They went inside and sat in the back of the packed church. Andrew looked around and recognized Monty, Daisy, Lenore, and several other townspeople. After the service, they drove down Liberty Street towards the cemetery, and were about to pass their homes.

"Would you mind if we left the car at your house and walked?" asked Gwyn. "It's only fifteen minutes or so down the road."

"Not at all," said Andrew pulling into his driveway. "Why is the cemetery so far from the church?" he asked as they got out of the car and sauntered down the street.

"There's one behind the church, but it was small, and they ran out of space, so they had to find a new plot of land, and this was the closest. It's owned and operated by the funeral home."

They walked into the cemetery just as the casket was being removed from the hearse, and quietly ambled behind it, then watched as it was placed at the gravesite. As Father Malcolm began the Rite of Committal, Andrew looked over at Edwin's parents and younger sister, and felt sorry for them. He also noticed many of the mourners were around Edwin's age, and realized he must have been well-liked. After saying the Lord's Prayer, grievers went over and offered their condolences to the family. When Gwyn returned, tears were streaming down her face, and Andrew comforted her.

"Hey, Gwyn," said Daisy in a shaky voice and drying her eyes.

Gwyn let go of Andrew and held her friend. After several minutes they separated.

"Are you coming to 'Edwin's Celebration of Life?'"

"Yes," replied Gwyn.

"Just to let you know, I've set up a private area for family and friends," she explained. "It begins in about an hour, but if you get there early, just grab a seat at the bar."

"Thanks, we will."

"I'm so glad you'll be there," she said squeezing Gwyn's arm. "You too, Andrew."

They said goodbye to her, and slowly walked out of the cemetery.

"During the Rite of Committal, when Father Malcolm was reading from the Bible, I was thinking about the people who have had these so-called accidents, and I started wondering if what has happened to them was such a bad thing. I know that's terrible to say, or even think, but those people weren't nice, and did some hurtful things to others," said Gwyn stopping and looking at Andrew. "Does that sound cruel?"

"During the service I was thinking the same thing, up until the very end."

"What changed your mind?" she asked curiously as they started to walk again.

"When I looked at his family, and I saw the pain on their faces, I started thinking about his parents putting money together to get him into rehab. And if he had gone, who knows, it may have turned him around."

"I never thought about it like that."

"It also got me thinking about Al Smith. His wife had called the police from her friend's house, and he was going to get arrested, charged, and do some jailtime. Maybe that would have shaken him up and made him realize he needed help."

"You're saying each of them deserved a chance to try to redeem themselves and shouldn't have been written off so quickly."

"I am, because 'trying is the only chance for success, where if you never try, you have already failed.' Oh my God!" said Andrew stopping in his tracks.

"What is it?"

"We have to go back to the cemetery."

Father Malcolm said goodbye to the last couple of people. Then the solitary figure walked over to his car, removed his gown, folded it neatly, and placed it on the front seat. He walked back to Edwin's grave and quietly prayed. In the distance, Andrew and Gwyn walked into the cemetery, up to the grave, and stood next to him.

"Your great-uncle said you were clever, and that it would only take you a few days to figure it out. Please, walk with me?" he asked, as they followed him. "Your great-uncle and I spent a great deal of time together talking about philosophy, we both took it in college, as did you, Andrew," he said stopping at his great-uncle's grave.

"Yes, I did, and my great-uncle and I, also talked about philosophy frequently."

"I know, he mentioned that to me on several occasions," replied Father Malcolm.

"I also know that you will not find the quote, 'trying is the only chance for success, where if you never try, you have already failed,' in any philosophy books. That was a quote my great-uncle made up."

"Yes, he did."

"I thought it sounded strangely familiar when you quoted it after Mass, but I didn't piece it together, until leaving here today," revealed Andrew looking at him. "My great-uncle spoke to you, didn't he?"

"He did."

"Did he tell you everything?"

"No, your great-uncle was very protective of me, and the parish. I am just the middleman, or perhaps, delivery man is a better term." The priest turned towards Andrew. "During the time your great-uncle was in hospital, I visited him almost every night, for an hour or two. We mostly talked about philosophy, about you, and the local news. Except for one night. He had a concerned look on his face, and I asked him if everything was okay, to which he replied no. He instructed me to go to the nursing station and ask them for a piece of letter size paper and two envelopes. I did as he requested and came back. On the piece of paper, he told me to write the following: the number one, and a name; the number two, and a name, and so on, till I wrote the number eight, and the last name. He then directed me to fold the paper up, place it in the envelope, seal it, and write the name 'Deputy Sheriff Williams' on it, which I did, then he signed it. Then he requested that I go to his jacket in the closet, take out the two small keys from the inside pocket, and bring them to him. Once I did, he told me to write your name on the envelope, put the keys inside, and seal it. Again, I did what he asked, and he signed it. Then he told me to go to his lawyers in the morning, hand them to him, and tell him his instructions."

"Instructions?" asked Andrew.

"Yes," replied the priest. "The first, was he wanted to make sure that when you were given the keys, that they were taken out of the envelope, and placed in your hand. The second, was that after you left the lawyers, the deputy sheriff was to come by and be given his envelope."

"Did he ever tell you about the names, what they meant, where he got them from?"

"No, he never did, so I never asked, and if he had wanted me to know, he would have told me."

Andrew looked over at Gwyn's stunned face, then back at Father Malcolm. "You knew what the keys were for?"

"I did," he replied.

"Then why the charade?" asked Gwyn.

"Andrew's great-uncle told me to be very careful, so for my own safety, I acted like I knew nothing."

"Did you know about the satchel?" asked Andrew.

"I did, but not its contents. I surmised it contained the same list."

"It did," confirmed Andrew, then paused momentarily. "When I asked about opening the satchel, you told me, 'Your great-uncle left that for you, and I doubt there is anything of value for the church inside. Please, take it and open it in the privacy of your home,' were those his instructions?"

"Yes, they were."

"And when you said, 'if you're great-uncle left that just for you, he meant for it not to be shared lightly, be careful who you show it to,' that was his warning?"

"Yes, it was, he wanted you to be vigilant," replied Father Malcolm.

"Andrew, why wouldn't your great-uncle just tell you what he knew?" asked Gwyn. "Why all this cloak and dagger stuff?"

"He was scared, just like you were, and like Father Malcolm is. I would bet, that under his breath, my great-uncle probably summed it up just like you did that morning outside the diner, well, minus the profanity."

Gwyn thought back to what she said, 'this is fucking creeping me out!'

"Andrew's great-uncle has taken every precaution to protect, not only himself, but me, the both of you, and the parish," stated Father Malcolm.

"I understand," said Gwyn, suddenly realizing the gravity of the situation.

"Thank you for your time, Father," said Andrew.

"Before you go, your great-uncle said that after you contacted me about the philosophy quote, I should tell you this."

"Tell me what?" asked Andrew.

"That, the boxes have ears."

"The boxes have ears," repeated Andrew. "I don't know what that means."

"Either do I," admitted the priest, "but your great-uncle said you would figure it out."

They said goodbye to Father Malcolm, left the cemetery, and walked down Liberty Street. Andrew knew that Gwyn was aching to ask him, and wondered how long she would wait before she did.

"Why couldn't your great-uncle just say what he meant?"

"Because he was scared, and worried, not only for himself, but for us," answered Andrew. "As surely as priests believe in God; they must also believe in the Devil."

"Oh, that's comforting!" said Gwyn.

Andrew put his arm around her, and she cuddled into him. "I think we need to have a little chat with our friend, Monty."

They arrived early, sat at the bar, and ordered drinks. Andrew spotted the deputy sheriff on the patio, nudged Gwyn, and they went outside.

"Good afternoon," said Monty. "That was a lovely service."

"It was," replied Gwyn, "and I think 'Edwin's Celebration of Life,' is going to be a fond way of remembering him."

"Me too," agreed Monty, and noticed Andrew was unusually quiet. "Looks like there's something on your mind?"

"Actually, there is."

"Well, let's hear it," said Monty leaning back.

"I wanted to ask you something."

"Please, ask away."

"It's about a letter size piece of paper that you have in your possession, which contains the names of eight people, seven of whom have died mysteriously over the last eight months."

Monty's grin quickly evaporated as he sat upright. "How on God's earth do you know about that? I haven't told a soul."

"Is that why you asked me for my help, so I could put the pieces of your puzzle together?"

"It's not like that," replied Monty nervously looking around. "We can talk about it, but not here, not now."

"When?" asked Andrew.

"Tomorrow afternoon at my place, we're having a BBQ. Come by for a beer, have some food, and meet the family, then we can go into my office where we can talk in private."

"Okay," said Andrew standing with Gwyn.

"They said you were very clever," said Monty shaking his head and smiling at him, "but now I see that was a gross understatement."

Chapter Thirteen

"Come in and take a seat," offered Monty, closing the office door behind him.

They watched him sit, remove the letter from an envelope, and hand it to Andrew. He quickly reviewed it, then passed it to Gwyn, who did likewise.

"How did you find out about it?" he asked interestedly.

Andrew told him about his discussion with Father Malcolm but not about the satchel. "What did you do after you received it?"

"After the lawyer handed it to me, I went to my squad car, and opened it," explained Monty. "You could imagine my surprise when I read the names."

"What did you do then?" asked Andrew.

"I contacted my associates in the city and they agreed to help me."

"How?" asked Gwyn.

"The accidents were happening numerically. I knew Emma Cooke was going to be next, so the city sent me a surveillance team. They watched the front and back of her house, and also bugged inside her home and listened in a white cleaning van across the street. Unofficially, of course."

"And after she was killed, you had them do a sweep of the house from top to bottom, looking for evidence," reconfirmed Andrew.

"Yeah," he replied. "I wondered if you'd caught my slip up the other day?"

"I did."

"I'm glad you're on our side," expressed Monty, then continued. "There was no evidence of anyone coming in or out, and our people watching, said they saw nobody. We did the same set up for Edwin Edwards, unfortunately, with the same result."

"You said you bugged their places, does that mean you have the recordings?" asked Gwyn.

"I do," replied Monty taking a flash drive out of his drawer and putting it into his laptop. "We placed microphones throughout the house and recorded everything. This is Emma Cooke just before she died, and trust me, it's going to sound weird, and be disturbing." Monty looked up at Gwyn. "Are you going to be okay with this?"

"I am," she replied.

Monty played the recording.

"Hey, Magic, what brings you up here?"

Magic meowing.

"Are you hungry, girl?"

Magic meowing.

"Why don't you jump up here onto the toilet lid and wait till I'm finished, then I will get you some tuna. How does that sound?"

Silence.

The sound of a hairdryer.

"Wait, what?"

Silence

"No, Magic, naughty cat!"

Silence.

"No! Please no!"

The splash of the hairdryer hitting the water.

The sound of electricity in the water.

Emma's body rattling off the tub.

Silence.

Monty stopped the recording.

"Poor woman," said Gwyn placing her hand over her mouth.

"The electricity didn't shut off when the hairdryer hit the water?" asked Andrew.

"No, it's an older house, and unfortunately the electrical outlet didn't have a GFCI," replied Monty sadly, then looked down at his laptop, and clicked on his keyboard. "This is Edwin Edwards," he said pressing play.

"Hey, Magic. What are you doing here?"

Magic purring.

"Do you want a hit little dude?"

Silence.

"Really?"

Silence.

"I must be pretty messed up."

Magic meowing loudly.

"Okay, kitty, I'll fix you up."

Silence.

"We're all good to go, little dude. Now all you need to do is put your arm like this."

Silence.

"I can't see any of your veins, so I'm just going to jab it in quick and hard, so keep still."

Short silence.

"Okay, on three…one, two, three."

Silence.

Edwin falling onto the floor.

Monty stopped the tape and looked at them. "Pretty strange, right?"

"Magic is the cat?" asked Gwyn looking at Andrew.

"He can't be," he replied. "There is no way he had time to be at Lenore's house, my place, and those houses."

"But they both called the cat Magic."

"They did," said Andrew thinking. Suddenly, he looked at Monty. "Can you play Emma's recording again?"

"Sure," he replied clicking on his keyboard. "Here it is."

"Hey, Magic, what brings you up here?"

Magic meowing.

"Are you hungry, girl?"

Magic meowing.

"Stop!" said Andrew, "rewind to the last part."

Monty did, and pressed play.

Magic meowing.

"Are you hungry, girl?"

"Stop!" said Andrew. "Emma Cooke called Magic, 'girl.'"

"So?" asked Monty.

"Magic is a male," divulged Gwyn.

"Maybe Emma's mistaken," suggested Monty. "Edwin called it, 'little dude.'

"If this cat was visiting these people, staying with them, and being caressed by them," stated Andrew. "I'm pretty sure, in the line of business Emma was in, she would be the one to notice what sex the cat was."

"What line of business would that be?" asked Monty.

"She was a porn star, who had a webcast site, where individuals paid a subscription to watch her…perform. And I'm sure, she would know the difference between a male and female."

"At your place, when I gave you the background information on the victims, I only told you she was a high-end call girl," said Monty, baffled.

"We'll get to that in a minute," replied Andrew. "You said you spoke with Jane Smith about the cat?"

"I did."

"Can you call her and ask if she knew whether the cat was male or female?"

"I can," said Monty picking up his cell and dialing. "Hello, Mrs. Smith, it's Deputy Sheriff Williams, sorry to bother you on a Saturday afternoon, but I just have a follow up question for you from the other day." Monty listened. "Thank you, this will only take a moment. The cat you told me about, Magic, do you know whether it was male or female?" asked Monty, then listened. "Are you positive?" he queried and listened again. "Thank you, ma'am," he said, and hung up. "She's one hundred percent certain, it was a female."

Gwyn glanced at Andrew with a relieved look on her face.

"You said something about a porn star?" asked Monty looking at Andrew, who turned to Gwyn.

"Here you go," she said handing Monty the documents and flash drive.

The deputy sheriff leaned back in his chair and flipped through the pages. "How did you come by these?"

Andrew told him.

"Did he mention where these documents and flash drive came from?" asked Monty.

"No, my guess is that he found the flash drive, looked at the files, then printed a copy of each," suggested Andrew. "Where he found the flash drive and who created the files, that's the mystery?"

"You know this is evidence."

"That is why we are giving them to you," acknowledged Gwyn.

Andrew quickly glanced at her and gave her a smile and a wink.

Monty let out a heavy sigh. "So, what does this all mean?"

Andrew and Gwyn briefly looked at one another, then Gwyn spoke. "We have a person or people, who have put together these documents, to act as the judge, jury, sentencing, and executioner of those individuals they feel deserve to die, and they are doing so, by using black magic to possess a stray black cat to carry out their executions!"

"I couldn't have summarized it any better myself," said Andrew proudly.

"Oh, and you're buying into what she is saying?" asked Monty.

"Of course, because right now, those are the facts," he replied, then paused briefly. "Monty, I could say something simple and straightforward like, what we are looking for is a stray black cat that researches, stalks, and kills individuals it doesn't like. But Gwyn would be quick to remind me that she may be naïve, and knows a cat is capable of doing many wonderful things, but that is quite a stretch."

Chapter Fourteen

"Here's your coffee," said Gwyn handing it to Andrew. "I'm just going to leave mine on the floor, here, next to my chair. I'll be back in a minute." She returned momentarily with a saucer of milk. "Here you go Magic, something for you, too." She picked up her coffee, sat on a porch chair next to Andrew, and watched Magic jump out of his basket, and lap up his milk.

"I think that cat is more here, than at home," said Lenore slowly climbing the steps and carrying a pie.

"Let me help you," said Andrew, putting his coffee down and walking towards her.

"This is for you, its chicken potpie."

"Thank you."

"You're very welcome."

"It looks, and smells delicious," said Andrew sniffing it.

"Well, you will have to let me know if it was, after you've tried some," said Lenore.

"I'm going to put this inside. Can I get you something to drink?"

"No, I'm fine, I'll just take a seat for a minute or two."

Andrew left, and when he came back Lenore was in his seat, so he picked up his coffee, and sat on the porch step facing them.

"We were just talking about how much Magic loves his milk," said Gwyn.

"He definitely does," said Andrew. "I hope you don't mind him being over here so much?"

"Not at all, dear," replied Lenore. "I'm out most of the day, and in bed early. He's probably lonely and likes your company."

"We also bought him some food and a basket," continued Andrew. "Maybe I should have asked first?"

"No, you go ahead and pamper him," said Lenore with a giggle. "He looks very content."

"Where are you going in your Sunday best?' asked Gwyn.

"We're playing euchre this afternoon in the church hall basement," replied Lenore. "I'm responsible for bringing one of the meals this week, so I made a chicken pot pie, and an extra one for you two. It gives us retirees a chance to get out of our houses, have a meal together, and to chat and catch up on the latest gossip. I hope you don't mind if I chitchat a little bit about you two?" she asked mischievously.

"Of course not," said Gwyn. "We would be hurt if we were left out of the town's gossip."

"Then I'll make sure I do," she said standing up and walking slowly to the steps. "I noticed the deputy sheriff here the other day, is everything okay?" she asked looking at Andrew.

"Yes, he just came over to say hello, welcome me to the town, and offer me his condolences again. He was one of my great-uncle's pallbearers."

"That's right he was, and it was such a lovely service," sighed Lenore, "and the one for Edwin, too. I thought the 'Celebration of Life' was a delightful touch."

"I couldn't agree with you more," said Gwyn.

"I really must be on my way, or I will be late, enjoy your potpie."

"Lenore, I meant to mention it to you earlier, but your pecan pie was delicious, the best thing I ate all day," complimented Andrew.

"Thank you, I took one of those with me last week to euchre, and it was gone in no time."

They watched Lenore slowly walk down the steps, get into her car, and drive away.

Andrew sat back in his seat. "What a charming lady." Noticing there was no reply from Gwyn, he looked over at her staring at him unamused. "What?"

"Best thing you ate all day?" questioned Gwyn. "If I recall, that was the same day we ate my homemade lasagna."

"You're right, it was," agreed Andrew finishing his coffee, putting the empty cup on the porch, and looking around nonchalantly. He could feel the glare from her stare. "I can't wait to try that chicken pot pie!"

"That's it, pal! Your ass is grass!" she said jumping on his lap and tickling his stomach.

"Okay, okay, I give in, you win," he said putting his arms around her.

Gwyn snuggled into him. "Did you really think her pecan pie was better than my lasagna?" she asked in a pouty voice.

"No," he replied.

Gwyn smiled.

"I think her pecan pie was a hundred times better than your lasagna."

"That's it, mister!" she said tickling him again. Eventually she stopped, looked at him, and kissed him full on the mouth, to which he reciprocated. Gwyn gently pulled away and put her head on his shoulder. "What do you want to do this afternoon? Should we take a walk downtown or to the beach, and give the townspeople something to mouth about?"

"Mouth about?" asked Andrew with a chuckle.

"You know, give them some gossip," said Gwyn sitting up.

"Okay, let's go for a walk, and give the townspeople something to mouth about!"

"You two are making this place your regular hangout," said Daisy. "Do you know people are talking about you guys?"

"I hope it's all naughty and sexy," said Gwyn impishly.

"Unfortunately, not," replied Daisy. "It's more on the lines of what an adorable couple you make."

"Oh damn!" said Gwyn disappointed.

"If you want, I can spread some juicy stories," suggested Daisy. "Do you have any?"

"We just had sex in the shower before we came out," said Gwyn to Daisy, before looking over at Andrew to see if she had been successful in embarrassing him.

"Oh, and don't forget last night on the porch swing," added Andrew.

"Andrew!" said Gwyn blushing.

"Now that's the kind of story people want to hear!"

"Daisy, you wouldn't?" asked Gwyn.

"Girl, you have the worst poker face I have ever seen."

"So I've been told," replied Gwyn with a laugh.

"Andrew, here, word of mouth is our communication tool, forget about all that texting and Facebook stuff. So don't be surprised if the townspeople start walking or driving passed your place at nighttime, trying to catch a glimpse of you two on your swing, doing your thing."

Andrew looked over at Gwyn. "Well, let's not disappoint them."

Gwyn tried to act shocked.

Daisy laughed at her friend's reaction. "Sure Gwyn, you're pretending to act all shocked, but meanwhile, you will be the one pulling poor Andrew out on to the porch swing!"

"I know," said Gwyn laughing with her.

Daisy stopped and gave her friend a startled look. "I'm actually surprised you haven't started to push me on my way, so that I can start telling people about your sexcapades."

"Start over there," said Gwyn standing, pointing, and giving Daisy a shove.

"Well, that's my cue, I'm off to go do some gossiping," said Daisy with a chuckle and departed.

"I can't believe you told her our front porch story," said Gwyn trying to be upset, but a little turned on. "What? I can see your mind turning."

"Sorry, it's nothing," he said, deciding he would tell her this evening, and went back to their conversation. "Gwyn, if we want to be gossiped about, we have to make it a really good front porch story."

"Andrew, in this small town, this will be considered a fantastic, mind-blowing, front porch sex story!"

Chapter Fifteen

"I'll have to admit it," said Gwyn following Andrew onto the porch and sitting in the chair next to him, "that chicken pot pie was delicious."

"It was."

"And we finished just in time to watch the sunset," she said with a smile as she sipped her wine.

"I love your smile," said Andrew admiring her. "Come over here." He reached out for her hand and guided her onto his lap.

"I'm liking this, more and more," she said cuddling into him.

They watched the sun slowly set, then the sky turning dark, and the stars appear one by one. Suddenly, Magic darted up the steps and leaped onto them, making them jump.

"Magic! "What's got into you?" asked Andrew.

"His heart's racing," said Gwyn stroking him.

"Maybe he ran into a raccoon. I'll go check it out." Andrew stood up, walked to the end of the porch, and looked down the side of his house. "I don't see anything."

Gwyn stood beside him holding Magic. "Look!" she said pointing.

Andrew followed her finger to a stray black cat scampering across Lenore's front garden, crossing the street, and down the side of a house.

"Do you think that's what spooked him?"

"I would say so," replied Andrew. "Do you blame him?"

"Not one bit," said Gwyn. "I'd be taking off in the other direction, too."

"I'm now convinced, that night we thought we saw Magic crossing the street and going down the side of Lenore's house, it was that cat."

"Me too," said Gwyn, feeling uneasy.

"Once it went into the backyard, where would it go from there? What's behind our houses?"

"Just a neighborhood: backyards, houses, trees, streets," replied Gwyn. "But if you walk down the street directly behind us, heading towards the cemetery, the road ends, and you come to the woods."

"The woods?"

"When the town approved the cemetery, they told the builders that there had to be woods between the houses and the graveyard. They didn't want people looking out their kitchen windows at graves."

"If you cut through the woods, do you arrive at the cemetery?"

"Yes, and the woods actually wrap around the back of the cemetery and continue on the other side."

"So the cat could take the backyards, starting from Lenore's for example, all the way to the woods, or through them to the cemetery?"

"It could," replied Gwyn. "Do you think that's where it lives, in the woods?" she asked, and then thought of something more disturbing. "Or the cemetery?"

"Maybe," said Andrew. "Let's go inside, get Magic some milk, and you some more wine."

"I know, I could use it, I'm a little freaked out!"

Andrew placed the milk-filled saucer on the kitchen floor while Gwyn poured them a full glass of wine. They went into the living room, sat quietly, and sipped.

"Are you okay?"

"Better now," she said lifting up her glass.

"I figured out something on that spreadsheet earlier today, when we were at Daisy's."

"You did. Why didn't you say something?"

"I thought about it, but I wanted us to enjoy our afternoon together."

"It was, wonderful," she cooed. "Perfect, in fact."

Andrew kissed her softly. "Yes, it was."

"So, tell me," she said anxiously.

"Before we left this afternoon for town, you said that it will give people something to mouth about, and explained that it meant gossip. I didn't give it much thought. But when we were talking with Daisy, she said to me, 'here, word of mouth is our communication tool,' on the spreadsheet, the word 'mouth' is in brackets, next to the descriptions."

Gwyn looked at him. "You're saying the word 'mouth' means gossip; people talking about other people's lives and secrets."

"Yeah."

"You are good."

"Thank you," he replied and noticed she was deep in thought. "You okay?"

She looked at him with a big grin. "I know how we can figure out when, and how, the information was collected on the spreadsheet," she said excitedly.

"You can?" asked Andrew.

"But I need my laptop," she said standing, heading to the door, and stopping.

"Actually, can you come with me?"

Andrew put down his glass and followed her out the door with Magic in tow.

"I guess he doesn't want to be on his own either," said Gwyn giggling nervously.

When they returned, Gwyn went into the den to set up her laptop, while Andrew went to the crisper and removed the plastic bag.

"Don't you feel guilty just giving Monty copies?" asked Gwyn glancing up.

"No, not really," replied Andrew. "He has what he needs for his evidence, and we have what we need for our investigation. Besides, I'll destroy ours once we've finished, and he'll never even know we had them."

"I'm ready," said Gwyn sitting back. "One summer job I had, was entering data into a program all day long, mostly numbers. Once entered, this data would then be transferred into charts and given to the sales managers to review. The data I entered was store sales versus online sales. Managers wanted to know information like, what times customers bought items in the store as opposed to online, what days had the highest store sales versus online sales, and so on. One day my manager needed some help, so she showed me how to transfer the data into charts, how to read them, and how to manipulate the data to create additional charts based on the data output required. So whatever the manager wanted, we could chart it, as long as the data or information was available."

"You're going to do something similar with the information on this spreadsheet?" he asked holding it up.

"Yes, I am!" she said happy with herself. "What I need you to do, is read out the information to me, so I can enter it."

"Okay."

"Go to the first person on the list, I don't need their name, just say number 'one,' and if they are highlighted, say 'blue.' If they have information under the 'Sins' heading, say 'box,' and tell me the day of the week it was entered, and if they have information under the 'Description' heading, say 'mouth,' and the day of the week that was entered. Then go to the next name, say number 'two,' and give me their information, then number 'three,' and their information, and so on, till you reach the last entry on the spreadsheet." She stopped and looked at him. "Does that make sense?"

"It does," he replied.

"They went through the spreadsheet and were done in ninety minutes.

"Okay, just give me a moment here?" she asked.

"I'll get us some more wine," said Andrew leaving, coming back with the bottle, and filling their glasses."

"Done," she said picking up her glass, leaning back, and looking up at him. "Since we are only interested in figuring out the correlation between the data and the individuals on the spreadsheet. What we want to find out is what days the information was collected on, the number of individuals on those days, and how it was collected," she said sipping her wine and leaning forward. "Look here."

Andrew stood over her shoulder.

"This is the bar chart with no data: the horizontal axis represents each day, Saturday to Friday; and the vertical axis, the quantities, or total number of entries for those days. Now, when I upload all the information," said Gwyn pressing the keys. "Voilà!"

Andrew looked on in amazement.

"This is the data for all the individuals. They either had information entered on the spreadsheet under the 'Sins' heading, which we identified as 'box,' or the "Description' heading, which we identified as 'mouth,' or under both headings. The biggest peak is Saturday, followed by mid-sized peaks on Sunday and Wednesday, and then small bumps for the remaining days," she explained.

"So, most of the information was collected on Saturday."

"Yes, but hold on," said Gwyn, "I can do better than that." She removed the data. "This new chart will show us the individuals that only had information entered under 'mouth.'" She pressed enter. "These peaked on Sunday and Wednesday, and have small bumps Monday, Tuesday, Thursday, and Friday, but nothing on Saturday." Gwyn clicked on her keyboard. "Now, here are the individuals that only had information entered under 'box,'" she said and pressed enter.

They both looked at one another with shocked faces.

"They only show up on Saturday," whispered Gwyn.

Andrew tried to wrap his head around it. "The data for 'mouth' was collected primarily on Sundays and Wednesdays, but on occasion, Mondays, Tuesdays, Thursdays, Fridays, but never on Saturdays, correct?

"Correct."

"The data for 'box' was collected only on Saturdays?"

"Yes."

"Can you chart only the individuals that had information entered under both 'box' and 'mouth'?

"I can," she said with a smile and clicked on her keyboard. "Here it is."

"It peaks on Saturday, has average peaks on Sunday and Wednesday, and has very small bumps on the other days," said Andrew. "I really don't see how this chart can help us because they're spread out."

"Well, they're spread out because it's a combination of 'box' and 'mouth.' We already know individuals with just 'box' only show up on Saturday; while individuals with just 'mouth' show up mostly on Sunday and Wednesday, but sometimes Monday, Tuesday, Thursday, and Friday."

"We do, keep going," suggested Andrew pushing her on.

"Hold on, let me think," said Gwyn smiling, sitting back in her chair, and sipping her wine. "I've got it."

"You do, already?" asked Andrew, impressed.

"Look at the total for Saturday. Now, combine all the totals for the other days," she said. "Saturday's total, and the other days' total, are the exact same. Which means that all these individuals have something in common on Saturday."

"What you're saying is, information was definitely collected about them on Saturday, and then additional information, or gossip, was collected randomly Sunday through Friday. So, Saturday or 'box,' is their common denominator."

"Yes," replied Gwyn.

"So why do some individuals share this common denominator, and others don't?"

"The person or people who created this spreadsheet, let's call them BM, used—"

"BM?"

"Black Magic," she said cheekily.

"All right, BM," said Andrew with a grin.

"BM used a template for their spreadsheet. When they updated it with an individual's name, that became part of their template. They would then add the information they had just found out about that individual, either under 'Sins' or 'Description,' and then enter the date they had heard it. For information entered under 'Sins,' the date entered was always a Saturday. If it was entered under 'Description,' the date entered would always be any day, but a Saturday. That's why some individuals share 'box' as their common denominator, and others don't, because BM has information about them under their 'Sins' heading."

"That makes a lot of sense," said Andrew, and thought momentarily. "Six weeks ago, they made the last entry on the spreadsheet, why do you think that is?"

"Thornton is a small town, with a small population, eventually you are going to run out of new people to add, or new information."

"True," said Andrew. "Which is probably why the status of the file was closed."

"Definitely, but what's more important, is that BM didn't stop updating the spreadsheet during the time the file was active. If any new information came to light for an individual, and it fell under a heading that already had information, they would just update it. If not, they would put it under a new heading."

"Are you saying, if they already had information under 'box,' and heard something about an individual, for example gossip, they would update 'word.' with that information."

"Exactly, and vice versa," said Gwyn. "If BM had information under 'word,' and then got some information under 'box,' they would update that. That's how BM ended up having individuals with data under both," said Gwyn.

"You're brilliant."

"Thank you," she said with a grin, then leaned over, gave him a kiss, and continued. "But BM's biggest mistake, and hopefully their ultimate demise, is that they were too meticulous with this spreadsheet. They updated the information on the exact day it was collected, and even categorized it under 'box' or 'mouth' leaving no room for error or inconsistencies."

"You're right, it is a big mistake, because this narrows down our search considerably. What we are looking for, is the relationship between 'box' and Saturdays; and where 'word' or gossip, takes place on the remaining days, specifically Sundays and Wednesdays."

"That's easy," said Gwyn.

Andrew sat back and crossed his arms. "This is definitely the 'Gwyn Show.'"

"The church hall," revealed Gwyn proudly. "Lenore only told us that seniors play euchre on Sunday afternoons, but it's a drop-in place for the whole community, and most of the town goes. They all bring a potluck, play games, watch sports on TV, but mostly chat and gossip. They even do the same thing on Wednesday evenings, except you are only allowed to play bingo, nothing else. It's a very big deal and taken very seriously. There's big money to be won. The last progressive jackpot, was one of the biggest, and was almost five hundred dollars!"

Andrew laughed and looked on admiringly. "Who would have thought my girlfriend was a computer geek?"

"Girlfriend?" she said playfully. "You're just my flavor of the month."

"Well, 'computer geek,' are you interested in going with your 'flavor of the month' to bingo on Wednesday?"

Chapter Sixteen

"Should I have brought something?" asked Andrew as they walked down Liberty Street.

"No," replied Gwyn. "Besides people think we're a couple, and if you brought something, they would think you don't like my cooking."

They walked into the church, down the stairs, and into the hall. Andrew followed Gwyn to the potluck table where she placed her blueberry pie with the other desserts.

"You better have a piece," she warned with a smile, "or else."

"Or else what?"

"It involves you, me, a bedroom, and you doing whatever I tell—"

"Good evening, Father Malcolm," said Andrew.

"Good evening, Andrew, Gwyn, nice to see you joining us."

"Thank you," they replied as he walked by.

"You could have warned me he was coming," whispered Gwyn.

"Where's the fun in that?" he asked with a puckish grin, as she gave him a playful shove.

"What are we looking for?"

"I really don't know, something out of the ordinary, maybe someone being very attentive," suggested Andrew.

"Someone taking notes or recording with their phone, would be a great lead," she said, "but that would be too easy. Apparently riddles, ambiguities, and anonymities are what we have to deal with."

"I do believe you are catching on," said Andrew, "and that you are starting to enjoy this."

"I must admit, I am," she replied, "except for the fuc…I mean, weird and creepy stuff."

"Look, there's Lenore with a group of seniors," he said spotting them. "Let's start there."

"Hi, Lenore, ladies, gentlemen," said Gwyn.

"Hello, Gwyn," they replied.

"This is Andrew," she said, introducing him around the table before taking a seat.

"This is the couple I was telling you about on Sunday, Andrew is my next-door neighbor, and Gwyn is his," explained Lenore.

"Oh, this is the adorable couple," said Beatrice.

"The ones that like to shower a lot together," said Jill.

"I heard something about a porch swing?" asked Fred.

"Oh Fred, you can't believe every rumor you hear, right?" asked Beatrice, as the group looked down the end of the table at the couple.

Gwyn turned to Andrew with a mortified look on her face.

"It's only a rumor if it's never validated," replied Andrew casually.

"So, is it a rumor?" asked Fred, as the group waited patiently for his answer.

"I'm afraid not," said Andrew, matter-of-fact.

"Good, it's about time this town had some spicy stories to talk about," said Jill.

Gwyn and Andrew listened to the group talk and joined in occasionally. Thirty minutes later the first game of bingo started, followed by another, then there was a break for people to grab some food. Gwyn introduced Andrew to another group of townspeople, and they sat with them for a while before moving on to the next. The last two games of bingo were played before the evening ended at eight. Gwyn and Andrew went to the dessert table, where Gwyn showed off her empty dish, along with her big smile. After which, they went up the stairs and left the church.

"I need a drink," said Gwyn.

"Yeah, I could use one too. Any suggestions?"

"There's a pub around the corner," she said, taking his hand and leading him to the front door.

Andrew looked up at its name. "The Olde Towne Fool."

"I'll tell you all about him inside," said Gwyn.

"He's an actual person?" asked Andrew, somewhat surprised.

They went to the bar, ordered their drinks, and sat at a booth that looked out onto Liberty Street.

"This is such a quaint town," said Andrew.

"You're starting to like it here."

"More and more each day."

She hoped he would consider staying for good.

"So, tell me about, 'The Olde Towne Fool.'"

"Okay, the story goes, that about thirty-nine years ago there was a very, simple middle-aged man who took all the money he had saved up, and inherited over the years, and bought hundreds of thousands of dollars in apple stock. When the townspeople heard he had bought stock in apples, they all made fun of him. They said they could walk a mile down the road and pick as many apples as they wanted from the abundant orchards for free. So, they nicknamed him, 'The Olde Towne Fool,' and deliberately spelt it wrong just to remind him how dumb he was. Well, twenty years pass, now it's August, 2000, The Olde Towne Fool says he's off to the big city to sell half of his stocks. A couple of days later, he comes back in a stretch limousine, wearing a designer suit. He tells everyone he bought a mansion in Palm Beach and is moving there at the end of the week. Eventually, the townspeople find out that the stock he purchased was for Apple, and that he had made millions. Before he leaves for Florida, he buys this place, turns it into a pub, and names it after himself. And tells the townspeople, that every time they walk through the town, they will always be reminded of The Olde Towne Fool. Apparently, he still owns it today."

"Is the story true?"

"Come with me," she said standing, "there's a portrait of him on the wall."

Andrew followed her and stopped in front of the drawing. It was a middle-aged man wearing overalls and a farmer's hat, with a straw in his mouth, holding up an Apple iPhone and taking a selfie, with apple orchards in the background.

"He's very subtle," said Andrew with a chuckle.

"Most definitely!" said Gwyn as they walked back to their table and sat. "To be honest, I don't know if the story is true, but it does add to the charm and character of this place."

"Whether it's true or not, I really liked it, and you're right, it does give this place its charm and character."

They ordered another drink, talked about the potluck and Gwyn's blueberry pie, then watched the waitress as she dropped off the pints of beers.

"Cheers," said Andrew as they touched glasses and took a sip.

"Bingo was quite a bust," acknowledged Gwyn.

"It was," said Andrew despondently.

Gwyn giggled at his look.

"What?"

"You seem so disappointed. What did you expect? Someone there to be wearing a pointy hat, with a wart on their nose, waving a wand, and then heading for home on their broom."

Andrew laughed at her cheekiness. "Sometimes I can be a little naïve."

She reached out and squeezed his hand tenderly. "I know most of the people in that hall tonight, many for a long time, and I can't see any of them being into black magic and possessing cats."

Andrew sighed and held her hand. "Is there another place on a Wednesday night where gossip runs abundant?"

"Not that I'm aware of."

"Then unfortunately, we have to face the fact."

"What fact?"

"We know BM has been collecting gossip about people on Wednesdays, and if that's the only place in town, it probably means one or several people there tonight, is BM."

"I never thought about it like that," said Gwyn, as a chill ran down her spine. "Do you think BM knew the reason why we were there?"

"I doubt it," he replied. "Hopefully they just saw us as a couple meeting the community."

"A couple," she repeated with a happy smile.

"Gwyn, I should come clean with you, your 'flavor of the month,' is only using this couple-thing for his cover."

"You are most definitely, a fucker," she whispered.

Andrew winked. "I will be tonight!"

Gwyn broke into a laughter. "On the front porch?"

"Are you guys going to do it on the front porch again?" asked Daisy.

"What are you doing here?" asked Gwyn excitedly.

"I left work early," she explained, "and I saw you two outside through the window, and thought I'd drop in for a drink."

"Are you on your own?"

"I am."

"Come sit with us," said Gwyn sliding over.

"What do you want to drink?" asked Andrew, getting the waitress's attention.

"Same as you guys," she replied.

"Oh, by the way, thanks for telling everyone about our shower and front porch escapades."

"You're welcome," she said laughing. "You two are officially the talk of the town."

"No thanks to you," said Gwyn.

"Oh yeah, like you're really upset about it," said Daisy rolling her eyes.

"Well, maybe not," said Gwyn as they both broke into a giggle.

"I heard you were at bingo tonight," revealed Daisy. "You two are becoming, quite the old, married couple."

"This town," said Gwyn shaking her head. "How did you hear about that already?"

"On the way here, I bumped into a group of seniors walking home, and they said you sat with them for a while. They told me that you were adorable, then asked me if I had heard about you guys in the shower, and on the porch swing. They asked me! I'm the one who started it," she said laughing.

Gwyn and Andrew laughed with her.

"Was it, Beatrice, Jill, and that group?" asked Gwyn.

"It was."

"Was Lenore with them?" asked Andrew.

"No, they said she left after bingo because she is covering reception early in the morning. Apparently, the other ladies don't start working at the church till later on."

"Working at the church?" questioned Andrew.

"They go in there a few times a week to clean."

"Clean?" asked Gwyn.

"They vacuum, mop, dust, clean the bathrooms, pews, and boxes," said Daisy sipping her beer.

"Boxes?" asked Gwyn.

"Yeah, the confessional boxes."

Gwyn and Andrew briefly looked at one another and smiled.

They spent the night talking with Daisy, then walked her home, before arriving at Andrew's porch.

"It's the black cat!" said Gwyn pointing as it crossed the street towards Lenore's place.

"Wait here," said Andrew giving it chase up the side of Lenore's house. By the time he got to her backyard there was no sign of it, and he slowly walked back.

"What was your plan, to tackle it to the ground?" asked Gwyn with a chuckle.

Andrew smiled back. "I just wanted to see where it was going?"

"And?"

"When I got to the backyard, it was nowhere to be seen."

"Possessed and fast; that's a deadly combination," teased Gwyn.

"Very funny," he said as they went inside and were greeted by Magic.

Chapter Seventeen

"We spent all last night at the bingo looking for something, lo and behold, in walks Daisy," said Gwyn as she drank her coffee.

"Confessional boxes, who would've thought," said Andrew shaking his head.

"What does it all mean?" asked Gwyn.

"It lines up with your data charts. All the information that was collected under 'box,' only showed up on Saturday, and confessions are only held on Saturday."

"Let me get this straight, BM is listening to gossip, mostly on Sundays and Wednesdays, and getting information, somehow, from confessions on Saturdays."

"Yeah," confirmed Andrew looking at her.

"I can't see Father Malcolm being BM."

"No, me neither, but unfortunately we can't rule him out," said Andrew, and then remembered something the priest had relayed to him from his great-uncle. "The boxes have ears," whispered Andrew, and thought for a moment, then looked at Gwyn. "The confessional boxes have ears!"

"What does that mean?"

"I don't know," he replied, as he watched the deputy sheriff pull up in front of his house, get out of his car, and walk onto the porch.

"Good morning, Gwyn, Andrew."

"Good morning," they replied as they watched him pull up a chair.

"I just came by to let you know that there's been no activity at Jean Laurence's place," he said taking off his hat. "Regrettably, the city wants to pull the surveillance. I asked them for another week, instead, they gave me four days, including today. Which means Monday morning they will be gone?"

"What happens then?" asked Gwyn.

"I will have deputies drive by every so often," replied Monty. "I don't have the resources to put someone on her fulltime."

"But she's in mortal danger!" stressed Gwyn.

"I appreciate your concern, but the people I have watching her now are doing me a favor, and a favor can't last forever," he explained. "This has all been unofficial, but now they have official work they need to do in the city."

"Can't you make this official?" asked Gwyn.

"And say what?" he asked. "Tell them, what you told me in my office. They would suggest I get a psychological evaluation, then tell me to take some time off, and get some rest."

"Andrew!" she pleaded.

"Unfortunately, he's right."

"I can't believe it!" said Gwyn, thinking he was going to support her.

"I understand what you are saying, and it concerns me too. But if you have something that you believe Monty's associates in the city would listen to, and actually believe, then share it with us."

Gwyn went quiet, Andrew was right, and now she felt foolish.

"Before I go, I did have a question about that spreadsheet."

"What is it?" asked Andrew.

"What do the words 'box' and 'word' mean?"

Andrew hesitated. "We don't know either, we've been trying to figure them out, and come up empty."

"Okay," said Monty standing. "If you do, let me know."

"We will," replied Andrew.

"Have a good day," said Monty looking at Andrew, then Gwyn.

"You too," replied Andrew.

Gwyn said nothing.

After they watched him drive away, Gwyn went inside, and Andrew followed her, and noticed she was crying.

"I feel like such a fool!"

"Why?"

"Because of what I said."

"Come here," he said pulling her close. "You said that, because you are worried for Jean Laurence's safety, and that's nothing to feel foolish about. I'm glad you did."

"You are, why?"

"Because now Monty has to deal with those men leaving, having limited resources, and you telling him that a woman is in mortal danger. He needs to come up with a plan to protect that woman. Otherwise, if something does happen to her, he will have to live with that for the rest of his life."

"You're saying I planted a seed in his head?"

"Yes, and I'm grateful for that."

"If I hadn't, would you have?"

"Without a doubt. I just thought it was more affective coming from you."

"A woman?" she asked.

"A woman worried about another woman's well-being," he replied. "Monty has a wife, and I'm sure he knows, she would be saying the exact same thing as you did."

Gwyn wiped her eyes and smiled at him. "You played the bad cop to my good cop, by asking me what I would say to his associates in the city, didn't you?"

"You are catching on fast, Gwyn," he said kissing her.

"I thought my silence was a nice touch."

"It was brilliant, and that sealed it for me."

"Why didn't you tell him what 'box' and 'word' meant?"

"He has enough to worry about with Jean Laurence's safety," he replied. "We'll concentrate on those."

"What's our next step?"

"My great-uncle has a bag of rosaries and wooden crosses, the kind they give to children when they are preparing for their first Communion. I think we should go give them to Father Malcolm, and at the same time, have a closer look at those confessional boxes."

Chapter Eighteen

Friday afternoon, they arrived at the church fifteen minutes earlier than scheduled, sat in a pew, and waited for Father Malcolm. Agreeing there was no one around, they left the bag, walked over to the first confessional box, and opened the door. Andrew quickly looked around inside, then did the same with the second one.

"I wonder what's on the other side of this wall?" he pondered.

"I think the reception area and offices," said Gwyn as she swiftly left, spied around the corner, and came back. "Yeah, it is."

"And underneath?" he asked, looking at her blank reaction. "Come on, follow me."

Gwyn trailed him to the basement, then into a storage room.

"They must be right above us?" he asked.

"I believe so."

"Run upstairs and go inside the first one and tap, then the second."

"Really?" she asked.

"Do you want me to go instead?"

Gwyn looked around the eerie storage room at the old statues and dusty religious paintings. "No, it's okay, I'll go." She left, knelt in the first box, and knocked loudly, then the second. She heard footsteps approaching and went quiet.

There was a knock on the priest's confessional door. "Hello?" asked a woman's voice.

Gwyn knelt on the small, cushioned pew. She heard the priest's door open and close, then listened as the small wooden door was being slid between the priest's box and the other confessional. Then nervously watched, as the wooden door between them slowly started to slide open.

"Gwyn!" said Lenore looking through the wooden lattice. "What are you doing in there?"

"I…I—"

"Lenore what are you doing?" asked Father Malcolm.

"I heard someone inside, and I came to ask them to leave," she explained. "It's Gwyn."

"Gwyn is here with Andrew to drop off some rosaries and wooden crosses," said the priest looking through the lattice. "Are you ready for me to hear your confession?"

"Yes, Father, I am."

"Thank you, Lenore," said the priest. "I will take it from here."

Andrew left the storage room, went upstairs unseen, and sat. Gwyn came out first, knelt in the pew in front of him, and said her penance. By the time the priest came out, Gwyn had finished, and he walked over to them. Andrew gave him the bag, and they talked momentarily about its contents, then left. On the way out, they bumped into Lenore.

"I'm so sorry about that, dear," she said, upset.

"Oh, it's quite all right," replied Gwyn. "I should have waited outside."

"I wouldn't have even bothered you," she continued, "it's just that I heard knocking sounds coming from them and went to investigate."

"I apologize," said Gwyn, "I was nervously tapping my foot on the floor."

"Not a problem, dear," said Lenore with a smile.

They said goodbye and walked outside.

"I don't know if Father Malcolm genuinely thought I was there for confession or came to my rescue," said Gwyn as they headed for home.

"I'm guessing the latter," replied Andrew.

"So?" asked Gwyn. "What did you find out?"

"I clearly heard your entire conversation with Lenore, and with the priest."

"You listened to my confession?" she asked embarrassed.

"Only the beginning, then I left. I needed to know if I could hear you when you were talking quietly."

"Does that mean that BM has been going down there and listening?"

"That was my initial thought," said Andrew, "then I wondered how they would know who the person was."

"Even if you knew everyone in town, it would be difficult to connect the voice to the person, especially when they are talking so low," said Gwyn. "Which means they would need to be watching them go into confession. But how could they be in two places at once?"

Andrew pulled his phone out of his pocket and played the recording of Gwyn knocking on the first confessional floor, then the second, followed by her conversation with Lenore, and the beginning of her confession. "I hit record and placed it on top of one of the beams."

"Very smart," she said with a grin, "and you're right, it's as clear as day. So, what are your thoughts?"

"BM gets there prior to the start of confessions, sets up the recording device, then goes upstairs, and makes notes of who is going in. Then later on, puts all the information onto their spreadsheet. The only problem, is that BM would need to know everyone in town."

Gwyn thought about what he had said. "Not necessarily."

"Go on," said Andrew, intrigued.

"If BM doesn't know them, they could just go up, introduce themselves, and find out their names before they left. They would only have to do it once."

"Great point," replied Andrew. "That means BM could be anyone in town."

"It does," agreed Gwyn.

"And there's no value in going to confession on Saturday to see if we can spot them, because they stopped updating their spreadsheet weeks ago."

"Still, they could be a creature of habit, and it may be worth having a look around," suggested Gwyn. "Besides, it's the only lead we have."

"Yes, it is."

"There is also another possibility," said Gwyn enthusiastically.

"What's that?" asked Andrew smiling at her.

"One individual could be listening or recording in the storage room, while another is watching the people going into confession. This would also support the theory, that there is more than one person involved," she said trying to hold back her excitement.

"That's excellent Gwyn!"

Chapter Nineteen

They arrived twenty minutes before confessions started, sat, and watched as people started to arrive. One by one the parishioners went into the confessional, came out, and said their penance. Some stayed, while others left. Gwyn got up, went to the foyer, and watched the ones that were leaving. Before they exited, Lenore handed them a church bulletin, and spoke with them briefly. Outside, Gwyn witnessed them either jumping into their cars or walking home. Eventually, she went back inside, and sat next to Andrew. After Mass, they walked hand in hand to Daisy's, and ordered a drink.

"Parishioners arrive, go to confession, some stay for five o'clock Mass, and others leave," said Andrew.

"Those that leave, are given a bulletin by the receptionist, then walk or drive home," added Gwyn.

"And those that stay, are given a bulletin after Mass, and say goodbye to the priest as they exit."

"Not much to go on," said Gwyn.

"No, not much at all."

Gwyn sipped her drink and thought out loud. "BM goes to church on Saturdays and records confessions, makes a point of meeting the people they don't know, then updates their spreadsheet. They also go to the church hall on Sundays and Wednesdays, meet people and listen to the latest gossip, then update their spreadsheet on those nights."

"What makes you say they are updating their spreadsheet on Sunday and Wednesday nights?" asked Andrew.

"Well, unless they're recording it, chances are BM would want to put down the information while it was still fresh in their mind, which would be that evening."

"They would, and like you said, their biggest mistake is that they were too meticulous with the spreadsheet," continued Andrew, following her train of thought, "so they would probably want to add it straight away, just to make sure it's accurate."

"Exactly!" said Gwyn.

There was a long silence while they both thought.

"What about the possessed cat?" asked Gwyn.

"I don't know about the possession-thing," replied Andrew. "To possess a cat would mean a person would have to actually take over the cat's mind and body," he explained, somewhat unconvinced. "But unfortunately, it's the only viable option we have at this time."

"Maybe it's not a possession," suggested Gwyn.

"What do you mean?"

"Perhaps it's more like a spell."

"A spell," repeated Andrew, thinking. "Do you remember Lenore had those books?"

"Yes, one was about magic, spells, and potions."

"We could ask her if we could borrow it?" suggested Andrew.

"Or we could just go to the library tomorrow morning, they'll probably have more books on the subject."

"That's a good idea," he said, then looked at her. "Why not just go on the internet?"

"Where's the fun in that!"

They walked home, and were about to go up the pathway, when they noticed the stray black cat on the other side of the road crossing over. Andrew put his index finger to his lips, then took off down the side of his house into Lenore's back yard, and waited. He eventually peeked around the corner but there was no sign of the cat. Andrew quietly went down to Lenore's front yard, walked across it to his porch, and met up with Gwyn.

"Where did it go?"

"You didn't see it?" she asked with a surprised look.

"No," he said somewhat mystified.

"Admit it, you missed it slowpoke," she teased. "By the time you got back there, the cat had already jumped the fence, and was halfway to its home in the woods."

"Or the cemetery," said Andrew in a scary voice, tickling her, and making her scream.

Chapter Twenty

They flipped through the fourth and final book.

"Nothing," said Gwyn shutting it closed and looking at Andrew. "Maybe we should talk to Lenore. She may be able to help us."

"I think we need to."

They arrived at her house as she was just getting back from Mass.

"Good morning, Lenore," they said.

"Good morning, Gwyn, Andrew."

"Can we have a few minutes of your time?"

"Of course," she said with a smile, "come inside and I'll make us some tea and sandwiches."

Gwyn looked at the pictures, and the books on the shelf, then sat next to Andrew when Lenore came into the room. She placed the tray on the table, and they took their cups of tea and a sandwich, and talked about the town as they ate. Once finished, Andrew brought up the reason why they were there.

"Last time we were here, we talked about the books you had on your shelf, about you growing up in Salem, and the popularity the subject of witches had on its residence, and the people who used to live there."

"Yes," she said. "I must admit I am a bit of an aficionado on the subject, I guess people today would call me a bit of a witch-geek."

Andrew and Gwyn laughed at her joke.

"Good," said Andrew encouraged by what she said. "Do you know if there is anyway a person can possess a cat?"

Lenore laughed. "I'm sorry, I'm not laughing at you, but the question. People like that, known by their more common name witches, don't exist and are fictional, so the question you are asking is quite academic in nature," she suggested. "But for argument's sake, let's say those types of witches did exist, they are notoriously known in literature for putting spells on people or giving them magic potions, not possessing animals."

"Could they put a spell on a cat or give them a potion to make them do something?"

"No, Andrew," she said shaking her head slowly. "In literature, a cat is a witches' dearest friend, she would never harm it or use it for malice. If I believed in them, I would say the way Magic is around you two, you could be witches," she said with a giggle.

"I guess you're right," said Andrew laughing with her.

Lenore sipped her tea and looked at them. "Can I inquire as to why you're asking these hypothetical questions?"

Gwyn nervously looked at Andrew.

Andrew quickly thought up a reason. "Well, I'm starting my next book soon, and I'm doing some research before I begin. I was considering having a villain who possesses a cat to commit murders. We looked through the books in the library but couldn't find anything on the subject. So, I thought I would pass it by you before I went in another direction with my storyline."

"Well, I'm sorry to disappoint you," she said sadly. "But for what it's worth, only because there's no mention of it, doesn't mean you can't write about it."

"Quite true," replied Andrew.

"Now, if you don't have any other questions, I need to excuse myself and get ready for euchre."

"I don't," replied Andrew standing. "Thank you for your time."

"Thank you," said Gwyn joining him. "Do you need me to help you carry these in?" she asked looking down at the cups and plates.

"No, dear, I will be fine, I like the exercise," said Lenore. "Are you going to the church this afternoon?"

"We are," she replied.

"Lovely, then I will see you both there," she said walking them to the door. "I know our group had a lovely time talking with you last Wednesday."

"As did we," said Gwyn.

They left and went to Andrew's house, where they were greeted by Magic, who rubbed up against Andrew's legs, then Gwyn's.

"You need to start charging him rent," joked Gwyn.

"No kidding," said Andrew laughing with her.

They went to the church hall for the afternoon, and afterwards, stopped in at The Olde Towne Fool for a drink.

"Someone or some group, that was there today is who we are looking for, isn't it?" asked Gwyn.

"It is," replied Andrew. He didn't want to scare her, but she needed to know. "There's a chance they also now know that we are looking for them, and if they didn't find out this afternoon, they will soon."

"What?" asked Gwyn alarmed. "How?"

"Lenore innocently told her group about me starting a new book, and the conversation we had with her about a person being able to possess a cat or put a spell on one."

"You should have told her not to tell anyone and to keep your story a secret."

Andrew didn't reply.

Gwyn looked at him prudently. "Wait, you wanted her to tell people."

"I did," he replied.

"Why?"

"To rattle BM's cage a little, maybe have them panic, slip up."

"Should I be worried?" asked Gwyn anxiously.

"No, I don't think so," he said calmly squeezing her hand. "BM doesn't want to reveal themselves to us, unless they have to, secrecy is their best ally."

"Good," said Gwyn somewhat relieved, then noticed Jill and Fred walking towards them.

"Hello, you two," said Jill. "Don't worry, we're not here to intrude on your evening, we just wanted to stop by and say hello before we sat down with our friends."

"That's very kind of you," replied Gwyn.

"I hear your writing a story about a villain who turns into a cat to commit murders?" asked Fred.

"Actually, he possesses a cat," clarified Andrew.

"Oh, my mistake," said Fred apologetically, "my hearing isn't what it used to be."

"That's okay."

"It still sounds like a good story," said Jill.

"Thank you."

"Well, we'll let you two get back to being a couple, have a nice evening."

"You too," they replied as they watched them leave and sit with another older couple.

"Daisy was right, word of mouth is definitely the communication tool for this town," said Andrew looking over at Gwyn who was staring at him. "Are you okay?"

"A villain that turns into a cat, I don't know what it is, but there's something to that."

"People can't turn into cats," said Andrew rationally.

"I guess not," acknowledged Gwyn, her enthusiasm fading.

They sipped their drinks and thought about it.

"But say, hypothetically, a person could. They wouldn't need to possess a cat or put a spell on it, they would become the cat, and they could easily commit crimes and would never get caught."

"It actually fits better into our scenario than the theories we currently have," said Andrew, "but like use said, it's hypothetical."

"I just thought of something else," said Gwyn. "Have you ever heard of ailuranthropy?"

Andrew shook his head no.

"Me neither, but Lenore had a book about it on her shelf, and I meant to ask her what it was about, but I forgot."

"When we see her again, we can," he suggested.

They talked for a couple of hours about Thornton, the townspeople, and its history. Every so often people would stop by their table and say hello. They eventually finished their last drink and headed for home, but when they arrived at Andrew's, they weren't greeted by Magic.

"That's odd," he said.

"Maybe he's over 'visiting' Lenore," said Gwyn humorously.

Andrew shook his head, pulled her close, and kissed her. "What am I going to do with you?"

"You know what I would like you to do," she said suggestively, and led him up the stairs.

Chapter Twenty-One

The following morning Gwyn came into the kitchen, poured a coffee, and sat next to Andrew. "I see Magic came back," she said spotting him eating.

"He was on the edge of the bed when I woke up this morning," replied Andrew. "I think something scared him last night, and he took off up to the room."

"He wasn't next door?"

"If he was, he wouldn't have been able to get into the house this morning, all the windows were closed."

"I wonder what frightened him?" asked Gwyn curiously.

"Come with me," he said.

Gwyn followed him into the den, and looked to where his finger was pointing, and noticed the satchel lock facing outward. "Did someone pick up the satchel, go through it, and mistakenly put it back facing the other way?" asked Gwyn, frightened.

"They did."

"And they came in when we slept?" she asked fearfully.

"No, all the doors and windows were locked when we went to bed," assured Andrew. "They came in before we got home last night, through the front door. I'd left it unlocked."

"On purpose?" she asked.

"They are going to come in anyway, what's the point in having them break down a door or smash a window."

"I guess," she said uneasily. "It was BM, wasn't it?"

"Yes, it was."

"They know we are looking for them?"

"They do."

"And you left them a secret recipe for grandma's chocolate chip cookies to read."

"We did," he clarified with a mischievous smile.

"Let's hope BM has a good sense of humor."

"Yes, let's hope so."

"Did you look inside the satchel?"

"No, I was waiting for you," he said picking it up and unlocking it. "Just the recipe."

"Should we have it checked for fingerprints?"

"We won't find any," he replied. "They would have worn latex gloves."

"Will BM come back?"

"No," he said confidently. "BM would have realized getting into the house, the satchel being left out in the open, and the keys sitting in the top drawer of my desk, was way too easy, and that we were expecting them."

"And the recipe," said Gwyn, "that was just to let BM know they wouldn't find anything."

"That, and now they know how to bake great chocolate chip cookies," said Andrew with a chuckle.

Gwyn giggled. "I don't know why I'm laughing; we just had a lunatic rummaging through our place."

"Our place?" asked Andrew, slowly walking backwards towards the door. "Maybe I should start charging you rent."

"You fucker," she whispered and chased him into the kitchen.

Andrew stopped, turned around, and Gwyn ran into him. He held her tight, kissed her, and she responded fervently. They eventually pulled away, smiled at one another, and sat at the table.

"What do you think our next step should be?" he asked sipping his coffee.

"The next time we go to the church hall, ask people to write down their 'Grandma's Secret Chocolate Chip Cookie Recipe,' till we get a match."

"Not a bad idea, but I don't think BM is going to fall for that," said Andrew with a snicker. "I think from now on, we don't share or ask people, for information."

"What about asking Lenore about ailuranthropy?"

"Let's look it up online first and see what we find out."

Andrew grabbed his laptop from the locked desk drawer, and placed it on the kitchen table, while Gwyn refilled their coffees. She sat down beside him, watched him type in 'ailuranthropy,' do a search, and pull up a website. After they both read it, they looked at each other in disbelief.

"A person who can turn into a house cat," whispered Gwyn, "also known as a werecat."

"I wonder why Lenore didn't mention this to us, especially with her having a book on the subject."

"Because you were only interested in someone possessing or putting a spell on a cat, not turning into one, maybe she didn't want to change your 'storyline,'" suggested Gwyn, poking fun at him.

"You're getting pretty witty," said Andrew glancing over at her.

"Thank you," she said tilting her head and giving him an endearing smile.

Andrew kissed her cheek affectionately, then went back to his laptop.

"I also got the impression from Lenore, that she thought it was all fictitious anyway, and didn't believe in any of it."

"I got that feeling, too," said Andrew. "Unfortunately, we don't have the same luxury as her, because we know differently."

"So, we are now looking for someone who can turn into a cat?" asked Gwyn, not believing the words were coming out of her mouth. "Then befriends its victims, stalks them, and kills them?"

"I believe we are," replied Andrew. "BM is the judge and jury, and the cat they turn into, is the executioner."

"Why did you have to say it like that, it freaks the fuck out of me!"

Chapter Twenty-Two

"Here's the chocolate cake," said Gwyn coming out on to her porch and joining Andrew.

"My favorite," he said taking the container from her and looking at it.

"I know, I remember you telling me, many, many, many times," she said playfully.

They strolled onto the sidewalk, held hands, and headed towards the church.

"I hope we have better luck at bingo this evening," suggested Andrew.

"With the progressive jackpot up for grabs at over six hundred dollars, the biggest it's been all year," she said melodramatically, "and we fill our card before the fifty-third number is called, it will be all ours!"

"Ha-ha," said Andrew giving her a nudge, "you know I meant finding BM."

"I couldn't resist," admitted Gwyn.

"You know, you're lucky I hang out with you."

"You're lucky I let you," she retorted quickly.

"I must admit, you're getting better with your comebacks."

"Of course, I am, I'm learning from the best," she said cheerfully. She suddenly stopped, took the container from him, placed it on a bench, and looked into his eyes. She had wanted to tell him so many times before, and hadn't, but for some reason, now just seemed like the perfect moment. "I really like you a lot, and I enjoy being with you, it's nice," she whispered putting her arms around him.

"I feel the same way," he replied holding her closely, and kissing her softly. "I can talk to you about anything and everything."

"Me too!" she said elatedly and giving him a radiant smile.

When they arrived at the hall, they went over to the dessert table. As Andrew looked around, Gwyn removed the cake from its container, and found a spot for it. Unexpectedly, Andrew felt her pulling on his sleeve, and looked over at her startled face. She pointed to a sign on the table that read, 'Grandma's Secret Chocolate Chip Cookie Recipe,' next to which was a paper plate full of cookies.

Throughout the evening, they casually asked people if they knew who had made the delicious cookies, but no one did. After the last one was eaten, the plate and the sign were thrown out by a volunteer.

"At least we know BM has a sense of humor," said Andrew as they left the church and made their way to Daisy's.

"It would seem that way," said Gwyn unamused. "Why do you think BM did that?"

"To scare us," replied Andrew bluntly. "Maybe scare us enough so that we would stop looking for them."

"BM was there tonight, watching us read their note?" asked Gwyn nervously.

"Yes, and we probably spoke to them."

"Them?" asked Gwyn.

"We can't rule out there may be more than one person involved."

"You're saying, BM meet, perform a black magic ritual, and then one of them changes into a cat?"

"It's a possibility that we can't ignore," replied Andrew, "although, I'm leaning towards it being just an individual, and maybe, an accomplice or two."

"Do you have any thoughts on who?"

"No, but one thing is for certain, they know we are close to catching them, and soon they will slip up."

"And we will be there when they do," she said confidently.

"Yes, we will."

Gwyn slowly stopped and looked at him. "Andrew, at the diner, I thought you were crazy for saying a cat was responsible for these murders. This week, I thought I was crazy for believing a cat was possessed. And this morning, I thought we were both crazy talking about a person changing into a cat. But with all the information we have uncovered, Monty's recordings, having someone break in, and BM leaving us a note, I have to say, this evening, I'm ninety-nine percent sure ailuranthropy is real."

"Not a hundred?"

"For me to be a hundred percent, I would have to witness a person transforming into a cat," acknowledged Gwyn, "and I know I will eventually, because that's the only way we will catch them."

"It is," he agreed.

"And if I were to tell my parents, family, and friends, all this, they would lock me up, and throw away the key."

"Yes, they would," he said holding her.

She held him tightly. "I'm glad I have you, it must be awful to know something like this, and not have a single soul believe you." She remembered back to him at the diner and glanced up. "Is it?"

"Sometimes," he replied moving her hair away from her eyes. "I'm just glad you made me agree to your one condition."

"Me too," she said kissing him wholeheartedly.

As they started to walk, he put his arm around her, and pulled her close. "By the way, your cake was delicious!"

"I noticed you cut quite a big slice," she said delightedly.

"I had to, I couldn't have the townspeople thinking I didn't like my gal's cooking," he joked.

Gwyn giggled and put her arm around his waist.

"I went back to have another piece, but it was all gone," he admitted disappointedly.

"Don't worry, one day I'll make one just for you and me," she said as she watched him open the door for her.

They had a couple of drinks, talked to Daisy for a while, before heading home. The sun had just finished setting when they arrived at Gwyn's front door. She quickly ran in, dropped off the container, and were heading to Andrew's when they spotted the stray black cat on the sidewalk.

They hid, and watched it cross to the other side of the street, then disappear down the side of a house.

"The other night, when I ran to the back of Lenore's to see where the cat was going, what time was it?"

"Midnight, maybe twelve thirty," guessed Gwyn. "Why?"

"Tonight, I'm going to do some surveillance of my own, in Lenore's backyard, and I'm going to follow that cat, and see where it goes."

"I'm coming too."

"But you can watch from the back-bedroom window," he suggested.

"No way," she said squeezing his arm, "I feel much safer with you."

At ten o'clock, Jean Laurence finished her bottle of wine, and looked at its empty contents; she was drunk but not too drunk to drive. She peeped out of her window at the surveillance car across the street, and decided her best option was to go out the back door, down the side of her house, and walk the length of her car to the driver's side door, rather than going out the front and across the driveway.

The two policemen noticed her walking down the side of her car, opening the driver's door, then stopping and looking down.

"Magic!" said Jean.

"Who's she talking to?" asked the policeman.

"I don't know," replied the other.

"I haven't seen you around here for a while. Did these policemen scare you off?" she asked as the cat purred and rubbed against her calf. "Do you want to come with me for a ride?" she asked picking him up and putting him on the driver's seat.

The cat jumped over to the passenger's and lay down.

"Was that a cat?"

"Yeah, it was."

Jean drove out of Thornton to the next village. "I have to go to the liquor store down in Dockside because Harry's in Thornton won't serve me if they think I've been drinking," she slurred looking down at Magic.

Fifteen minutes later she pulled up in front of the store, put on a wig and sunglasses, and went inside.

The two policemen looked at one another.

Jean got back in the car, put the bottles of wine on the passenger side floor, before taking off her disguise, throwing it in the back seat, and driving for home. She looked over, noticed Magic was gone, and wondered if the cat had jumped out when she'd opened the door. "Stupid cat," she mumbled. As she got close to Thornton, she looked in the rearview mirror at the car following her, and suddenly noticed the black cat sitting in the back seat. "Oh, there you are. I thought you had abandoned me," she muttered. The cat hissed and leapt onto her head causing Jean to swerve back and forth. She desperately tried to grab the cat as it moved down onto her face blocking her view. As she did, her foot pressed down on the gas, and the car accelerated. Jean swerved off the road, onto the shoulder, and sped down a steep incline. The cat looked at the tree quickly approaching and jumped for cover in the back. The last thing Jean saw was the windshield, then the tree; and the last thing she heard, was the sound of her spine snapping as she hit it. The black cat slowly jumped onto the driver's seat, went out through the broken windshield, and strolled along the hood. It stopped, stared into Jean's vacant eyes, then took off into the woods.

At eleven thirty, Andrew and Gwyn went into Lenore's backyard, and positioned themselves where they could see the cat come up the side of the house towards them, and pass by, without it noticing them. An hour passed.

"Maybe we should try again tomorrow night," suggested Andrew, starting to get up.

"Look!" whispered Gwyn pointing.

They watched the black cat cross the road, slowly stroll along the side of the house, stop, and look around. Suddenly, it jumped up onto a window ledge, and went inside. They looked at one another, then slowly crept to the window, and peeked in.

On the floor, was a black rectangular rug with a large red pentacle design, and on each of its four corners was one unlit candle. The cat leisurely strolled onto the rug, lay in the center of the pentacle, and slowly transformed into Lenore, as the candles mystically lit. Lenore stretched her naked body, stood up, put on her robe, and walked towards the window. They ducked down, and slowly backed away. With her hand guiding her along the wall, Gwyn felt the drainpipe, and went around it. She tried to warn Andrew, but was too late, and watched him bang into it. They quickly ran to the back of the house and hid behind the deck. Lenore stuck her head out the window and carefully looked left then right, before going inside and blowing out the candles. They could hear her coming towards the back door, and watched as the deck light came on. They raced down the side of Lenore's house, across her front yard, to Andrew's porch, and into his home. Lenore came out onto her deck with a flashlight, shined it down the side of her building, then into her backyard, and spotted a raccoon scurrying away from it.

Out of breath, Andrew and Gwyn collapsed on the couch.

"Lenore is BM!" said Gwyn shocked. "She seemed like such a sweet, old lady."

"I can't say I saw that coming," admitted Andrew.

"What are we going to do?" asked Gwyn looking over at him.

"I don't know."

Chapter Twenty-Three

At eleven o'clock in the morning, there was a knock on the door, and Gwyn opened it.

"Hi, Monty."

"Hello, Gwyn," he replied solemnly. "Is Andrew with you?"

"I am," he said walking up behind her.

"Do you mind if I step in for a moment?"

Monty came inside and told them about Jean Laurence. "So, in summation, she was intoxicated, lost control of her vehicle, went down an incline, and crashed."

Gwyn looked over at Andrew horrified.

"You mentioned the policemen saw a black cat?" asked Andrew.

"Officially, they witnessed Jean picking one up and putting it in the car. Unofficially to me, before the crash, they said it looked like she was struggling with something on her head while she was driving. They were too far behind, said it was dark, and therefore couldn't make a positive ID. They also said it was possible she may have been having some kind of hallucination and was just grabbing at her hair. I asked if they had to hazard a guess as to what it was, they both thought it was the cat. There was no cat at the crash scene."

"Did you find any scratch marks on her face?" asked Gwyn.

"She was pretty cut up from going through the windshield, and hitting the tree, so we're waiting to hear back from the coroner," he replied. "But we did find black cat hair on her clothes, the passenger seat, and the backseat."

They both knew the cat was Lenore, and were silent, then realized if neither of them said anything soon, Monty would suspect they were hiding something.

"She had surveillance, and still that horrible accident happened, but I guess they really couldn't have done anything," said Gwyn sadly shaking her head, then realized something. "Wait, I thought her surveillance ended last Monday?"

"After we spoke, the following day I talked to my associates in the city and showed them the anonymous letter I had received with all the names listed on it. They agreed to keep the surveillance going for another couple of weeks," he explained. "Not that it did her much good."

"You couldn't have done any more for her," acknowledged Gwyn sympathetically, "and I don't believe anyone could have."

"Maybe," he replied. He wondered if they knew something and thought about asking them, instead, he decided to let it go, and wait for the coroner's report. "Well, I just wanted to drop by, and tell you both firsthand what happened."

"Thank you, we appreciate that," said Andrew standing with him.

"We do," agreed Gwyn, as she got up and walked with them to the door.

"If you find anything or come across something, that can help me out with my investigation, please let me know."

"We will," they replied going onto the porch.

They watched Monty saunter down the steps, get into his cruiser, and leave.

"Do you think he believes we know something?" asked Gwyn.

"Probably," surmised Andrew, "but he's not going to ask us any questions, till he's got the information to back them up."

"He's not going to like what we found out."

"Hopefully, we won't have to tell him."

"What do you mean by…?" said Gwyn stopping, as she spotted Lenore driving up the street, and pulling into her driveway. "Perfect timing!" said Gwyn confrontationally.

Andrew tried to stop her, but she pushed his hand to one side, and went over.

"Why?" asked Gwyn upset. "Why are you killing these poor people?"

"So, it was you two snooping around my house last night," she said looking at them, "I thought it was." She calmly picked up her bag of groceries, closed the door, and went inside her house before coming out emptyhanded. "Cup of tea?" she asked.

They walked over and followed her inside. Gwyn took her phone out of her back pocket, placed it face down on the coffee table, then sat on the couch next to Andrew and waited. Lenore came into the parlor, poured the tea, and gave them each a cup.

"Why? Because these people hurt others and are scum," said Lenore candidly. "I thought you would be happy to be rid of them?"

"Happy?" questioned Gwyn.

"I'm sure Jane Smith is happy her husband had an accident. If she had not gotten out that night, he would have killed her. Who would you rather be alive today, her or him?"

"But she had called the police, he would have been arrested, and gone to jail," stated Gwyn.

Lenore laughed. "And then what? A few months later, he's out on good behavior, goes home, and picks up where he left off."

"Maybe she would have left him, maybe prison would have changed him, or maybe they would have sent him to see someone to get help."

"Maybe, maybe, maybe," repeated Lenore singing it like a song, then stopped. "He was never going to change, dear."

"What about the others?" asked Andrew. "They had no chance for redemption either?"

"No, they didn't," said Lenore casually sipping her tea.

"Edwin Edward's parents were going to put him in rehab."

"Can you listen to yourself Andrew?" she said shaking her head. "That boy was responsible for murdering three teenagers and almost a fourth. What about them? What about their redemption? How many teenagers are hooked on drugs because of Edwin Edwards? And how long do you think it will be before another one dies of an overdose from the drugs he supplied?”

Andrew and Gwyn were silent.

“Look at Jean Laurence driving drunk all the time,” continued Lenore. “How long are you willing to wait till she kills another innocent child?”

“But who gives you the right to be judge, jury, and executioner?” asked Gwyn.

“My birthright does,” replied Lenore, “and the birthright of my mother, my grandmother, my great-grandmother, and all my mothers’ before her.”

“Birthright?” asked Gwyn confused.

“Each of us has one special thing in common?”

“You’re all witches,” answered Andrew.

“Yes, we are all witches,” she confirmed with a pleasant smile.

“When you travel to each town, is this what you do?” asked Gwyn. “Research who the bad people are, stalk them, and then make it look like they had accidents?”

“Yes, my dear,” she replied honestly. “I find the church to be the most valuable wealth of information.”

“Do you always listen in on confessions?” asked Gwyn.

“Of course, in most of these towns the churches are quite old and have lots of nice nooks and crannies between the beams for me to hide my recording device. If that fails, placing one inside the confessional is my next best option. Then there are the town’s hot-gossip spots, it could be the church hall, the diner, or the local bingo hall. It’s amazing what people will tell you.”

Gwyn shook her head in disgust.

“Is there a reason why it’s eight?” asked Andrew.

“Eight is not a significant number,” she replied, “it can be as low as zero but can never be any higher than ten, and it has to be done within twenty-four months or less.”

“Why no more than ten, and within two years?” asked Andrew.

"Well, ten accidents over two years doesn't arouse too much suspicion, and the longer you stay, the more likelihood there is of you being found out," she explained. "Although, I must admit, you two were quite the exception, and I enjoyed it immensely. I thought the cookie recipe was a nice touch."

"You think this is a game?" asked Gwyn incensed.

"Oh no, dear, not at all," she replied sincerely, "but you two pursuing me was. When I realized someone was hunting me down, I had to finish my work here quicker than anticipated. Jean Laurence was most challenging, with her being watched constantly, and having her windows closed all the time. You see, once we pick our list, they all have to be taken care of, and we can't leave any loose ends."

"What about us?" asked Andrew.

Lenore gave them a long look before answering. "There is no need for me to change into a cat anymore, which means that you can't trap me. And nobody is going to believe you, when you tell them that a sweet old lady turns into a cat and kills people. Therefore, you give me no reason whatsoever for concern. And tomorrow morning, a moving truck will come here, pack up my things, and I will follow them to my next town." She stood up, went to the bookshelf, and pulled out a binder. Then took a piece of paper from her drawer, and quickly showed it to them; it was the list of the eight names from Thornton. "I was clumsy and lost my flash drive at the church. I went back to look for it, but couldn't find it, and assumed your great-uncle had. I knew he had viewed its contents, and eventually gave it to you. But I had nothing to worry about, because there was nothing on it that would link it back to me. Plus, the files were only copies, luckily, I had the originals on my laptop," she explained, then looked at Andrew. "I'm guessing the flash drive, a copy of this list, and probably the spreadsheet, were in the satchel?"

"They were," replied Andrew as they watched her put the list inside the binder.

"Is that the lists of names from all the different towns?" asked Gwyn.

"Yes, my dear," said Lenore fanning through all the pages, before putting it back on the shelf. "Now, I have things I need to do before the move tomorrow. Do you have any more questions?"

"How do you change into a cat?" asked Andrew.

"Ah, that's a good one, I'm glad you asked," she said taking a seat. "We lay down our ceremonial pentacle rug, which by the way has been in my family for centuries, then place four candles on each of its corners, and light them. We undress, sit in the middle of the pentacle, and cast our black magic spell. Once we've changed into a cat, the candles go out, and off we go to do our work," she said with a smile. "And as you both witnessed last night, when we return, we sit in the middle of the pentacle, transform back, and the candles relight."

"And you only perform it in the evening, preferably after sunset, but you need to return before sunrise," added Gwyn.

"I must admit, you two make quite the pair of detectives, and I fear if I still had several victims left, I would have had quite the challenge on my hands," she said admiring them and standing up.

"Earlier, you said, 'we pick our list,' and 'we can't leave any loose ends,' are there more like you?" asked Andrew.

"When I said 'we,' I was referring to my ancestors, and I'm afraid I am the last of my kind," she said sadly. "But I do plan on living a very long and productive life."

"So, Magic," said Gwyn, "he's just a decoy?"

"I like you two very much, you have such intriguing questions," she said smiling and sitting down again. "Yes, he is. Locals say they see him around town, when in actuality it's me, which allows me to roam freely at my will. And when I move from a town, the cat that I had brought with me, I leave there. That way it doesn't raise any suspicion when they don't see a black cat running around anymore. Usually, I put it in a carrier along with a note and place it on the front doorstep of a young family. But since Magic has taken such a liking to you two, I was wondering if you may want him? If not, I can give him to someone else."

"We'll take him," replied Andrew without hesitation.

"Perfect," said Lenore clasping her hands, "that makes me very happy."

"Where did you get Magic from?" asked Gwyn.

"An animal shelter, and in a couple of days, I will pick out another one from there to replace him," she replied, and studied them briefly. "Do you have any further questions?"

They shook their heads no.

"If you will excuse me, I have things that need to be done before my move tomorrow."

Gwyn picked up her phone, then stood with Andrew, and followed Lenore to the front door.

"If you do find out where I moved to, and follow me there, I will add your names to my list, and you will both have life-ending accidents," she said uncompromisingly. "But I beg of you, please don't, I have grown very fond of you both."

They left her house, silently walked over to Andrew's, and went inside.

"Not only is she a witch, that can turn into a cat, but she's also fucking insane!" stated Gwyn turning to Andrew. "We can't let her leave!"

"No, we can't."

"What are we going to do?"

"Did you record everything?"

"I did," replied Gwyn lifting up her phone.

"Good, I have an idea."

Chapter Twenty-Four

At 5 p.m. there was a knock on the door.

"Lenore!" said Andrew surprised.

"I came over to say goodbye and thank-you for being such lovely neighbors. I also wanted to make you a peace offering with this apple pie, and there is fresh whipped cream in this container," she said smiling and lifting them up.

Andrew turned to Gwyn, who was now standing next to him, and they both looked at the pie.

"Oh, don't worry, there's no spell on it or magic potion in it," she said with a chuckle. "I even included a thank-you note, in which I mention giving you the pie, just to make you feel more at ease."

Andrew opened the door, took the pie, and the note, while Gwyn took the container.

"Now, I must be off, I have to say goodbye to my friends and drop some pies off for them too."

Andrew and Gwyn thanked her, said goodbye, watched her get in her car, and drive away.

After dinner, they cut the pie up, added generous heaps of whipped cream, and ate it in front of the kitchen window as they talked. Peeking through hers, Lenore vigilantly watched them devouring her dessert.

Just before sunset, Lenore went over to Andrew's, and placed a carrier and an envelope by the front door. Shortly after, Andrew heard Magic meowing, went out to the porch, and found him in the carrier. He picked it up, brought it inside, and placed it on the living room floor.

"What's this?" asked Gwyn.

Andrew opened the envelope and read the note. "Dear Andrew and Gwyn, as we agreed, here is Magic. I know he will be happy living with you in your home, and that you two will take exceptionally good care of him. Thank you, Lenore." He placed the note back in the envelope and looked at the cat.

"Are we sure it's Magic and not Lenore?" asked Gwyn closely looking at it.

"He's wearing his collar, so it's probably him," replied Andrew. "But without us taking him out of the carrier, and physically checking, there is only one other way to know for certain." Andrew left, returned a few minutes later with a bowl of milk, and placed it inside the carrier. "Magic loves his milk, and Lenore doesn't, she only likes cream."

"You're so smart!"

"I know," he replied with a cheeky grin.

They sat on the couch and watched Magic finish every drop.

"It's him," confirmed Andrew and opened the carrier.

The cat leisurely strolled out, slowly circled the room, then stopped in front of them, arched its back, and hissed.

"I don't think that's Magic!" said Gwyn.

"Of course it isn't," snarled Lenore. "You two think you are so clever, and yet, look how easy it was for me to get into your home. Did you honestly think I would leave without taking care of you two first?"

"No loose ends," suggested Andrew.

"Exactly!" chattered the cat.

"You must have hated lapping up that milk?" asked Gwyn.

"I did," she snarled, "but it was worth it."

"What are you going to do with us?" asked Andrew.

"The pie and whipped cream contained finely crushed sleeping pills," chirped Lenore, "and in a few minutes you will become quite tired and drift off to sleep. After which, I will knock one of those lit candles onto the couch, and another, under the curtains. Then I will leave by that open window, and watch from my kitchen, as you and your house burn to the ground."

"You're a very sick person!" said Gwyn.

"There's no need for name calling, dear, you're just upset because I outsmarted you both," she purred as she licked her paw, wiped her face, and waited for the sleeping pills to kick in.

Andrew politely cleared his throat to get her attention. "Lenore, you may want to take a look at what's on the dining room table."

The cat quickly leapt up, looked at her full pie and container of whipped cream, then turned around and growled at them before jumping down. She was starting to feel dizzy and losing her balance.

"We know you had put something in the pie, or whipped cream, or both," said Gwyn leaning over with a smile. "After you left, we went to the grocery store, and bought replacements. Then we purposely ate them in front of our kitchen window, and in full view of your peering eyes."

Lenore was now staggering.

"Oh, and the milk," said Andrew taking over, "contained a couple of tablespoons of nighttime sleep-aid liquid, giving it a somewhat subtle berry flavor. Which, with the amount you have ingested and your small frame, should kick in quite soon."

"No!" hissed Lenore. "What are you going to do with me?" she asked, and tried to come at them, but tripped over her paws. She attempted to get up, only to stumble, and fall back onto the floor. Lenore lay there panting heavily for a few moments before falling into a deep sleep.

Just before sunrise, Andrew and Gwyn put on latex gloves, and went over to Lenore's carrying a small filing cabinet. Andrew went in through the open window and unlocked the back door. They carried the cabinet into the room containing the ceremonial rug and candles, put it in the corner, then located the items in the parlor, and put them inside the cabinet and locked it. Andrew went back to his house and returned with the carrier containing the sleeping cat, and a black bag over his shoulder. He took the cat out and placed it in the middle of the pentacle, while Gwyn found Magic, and waited outside. Andrew put the carrier and collar in the parlor, then opened the doors to all the rooms and closed the windows, except for the room where the cat was laying. He opened his black bag, placed the container of whipped cream and Lenore's notes on the kitchen counter, then positioned the apple pie in the oven, and turned on the gas. Andrew picked up his black bag, closed the locked door behind him, and walked with Gwyn and Magic back to his place.

The gas slowly filled the rooms.

The black cat lethargically woke up, and gradually transformed into Lenore, as the candles mystically lit. Lenore stretched, put on her robe, and closed the window. She turned around, looked curiously at the new filing cabinet, strolled over, and studied it. She desperately tried to remember how the cabinet had gotten there, then tried to recollect what had happened before she had fallen asleep. Suddenly, she smelt something coming from the other side of the door, opened it, and realized too late what it was. The gas quickly filled the room, was ignited by the candles, and in minutes the house was engulfed in flames. By the time the fire department arrived and put it out, there was nothing left but rubble and ash.

The moving truck, never showed up.

Chapter Twenty-Five

The following Saturday, Andrew and Gwyn were sitting on the porch swing when the deputy sheriff pulled into the driveway. They watched as he climbed the steps, took off his hat, and sat in a chair next to them.

"Good afternoon," said Monty.

"Afternoon," they replied.

"We've finished our investigation into what happened next door."

"What did you find out?" asked Gwyn interestedly.

"Her death was accidental," confirmed Monty. "Looks like she was baking, the pilot went out, gas filled her house, and was ignited by a candle. Apparently, the oven she was using was an older model, and had a faulty pilot light."

"Poor lady, that's such a shame," said Gwyn.

"Yeah, it is," he said glancing over at the remaining structure and debris, then back at her. "Not much of the place left."

"No," she concurred.

"We did manage to salvage a fire-proof cabinet that was still intact. I finally got that opened yesterday and went through its contents."

"Anything of interest?" queried Andrew.

"A number of items," he replied, "some of them you two may find intriguing."

"Like what?" asked Andrew.

"For starters, she had a few books on magic, and one in particular caught my attention, it was called 'Ailuranthropy.'"

Gwyn glanced over at Andrew then the deputy sheriff. "What's that?"

"Basically, a person who can transform into a house cat, also called a werecat."

"Werecat!" said Gwyn giving Monty an odd look. "Do you think she was one?"

"At first, I would have said no, but there is a recording of her saying that she was, amongst other things."

"A recording?" questioned Andrew.

"It's mostly snippets of dialogue," he explained. "I'm guessing she recorded herself talking, then went back, and edited it. Which is why there are pauses in between, and it jumps from topic to topic. Her voice is normal, but what she is saying is very irrational, making me question her state of mind."

"Really!" said Gwyn surprised. "What does she say on it?"

"Quite a lot," replied Monty. "Unofficially, I'm taking it to be her confession."

"Her confession!" they said in unison.

"Putting her questionable state of mind aside. She reveals several details key to our investigation, which aren't public knowledge, and openly admits to the crimes she has committed."

"What are the details and crimes?" asked Andrew curiously.

"Here, listen, and you two can decide for yourselves," suggested Monty reaching for his phone, and pressing play.

"Because these people hurt others and are scum. I thought you would be happy to be rid of them?...I'm sure Jane Smith is happy her husband had an accident. If she had not gotten out that night, he would have killed her. Who would you rather be alive today, her or him?...A few months later, he's out on good behavior, goes home, and picks up where he left off...He was never going to change...That boy was responsible for murdering three teenagers and almost a fourth. What about them? What about their redemption? How many teenagers are hooked on drugs because of Edwin Edwards? And how long do you think it will be before another one dies of an overdose from the drugs he supplied?...Look at Jean Laurence driving drunk all the time...How long are you willing to wait till she kills another innocent child?...My birthright does, and the birthright of my mother, my grandmother, my great-grandmother, and all my mothers' before her…Each of us has one special thing in common?…We are all witches…I find the church to be the most valuable wealth of information.…In most of these towns the churches are quite old, and have lots of nice nooks and crannies between the beams for me to hide my recording device. If that fails, placing one inside the confessional is my next best option. Then there are the town's hot-gossip spots, it could be the church hall, the diner, or the local bingo hall. It's amazing what people will tell you."

Monty paused the recording.

"I see what you mean by her being very irrational, and questioning her state of mind," said Andrew shaking his head. "Is that how she collected the information for her spreadsheet, at the church, and hot-gossip spots?"

"I'm afraid so, but there's more," replied Monty and pressed play.

"Eight is not a significant number, it can be as low as zero but can never be any higher than ten, and it has to be done within twenty-four months or less…Ten accidents over two years doesn't arouse too much suspicion, and the longer you stay, the more likelihood there is of you being found out…Jean Laurence was most challenging, with her being watched constantly, and having her windows closed all the time. You see, once we pick our list, they all have to be taken care of, and we can't leave any loose ends…Tomorrow morning, a moving truck will come here, pack up my things, and I will follow them to my next town."

Monty paused it. "This next part is very disturbing," he warned, then pressed play.

"We lay down our ceremonial pentacle rug, which by the way has been in my family for centuries, then place four candles on each of its corners, and light them. We undress, sit in the middle of the pentacle, and cast our black magic spell. Once we've changed into a cat, the candles go out, and off we go to do our work…when we return, we sit in the middle of the pentacle, transform back, and the candles relight."

Monty paused the recording. "Weird, right?"

"That's an understatement," said Andrew. "Is she actually saying, she changes into a cat?"

"Yes, she is," confirmed Monty. "And when she says, 'off we go to do our work,' she means, off she goes to commit a murder."

"Murder!" repeated Gwyn shocked.

"This is the last piece," said Monty pressing play.

"When I said 'we,' I was referring to my ancestors, and I'm afraid I am the last of my kind…Locals say they see him around town, when in actuality it's me, which allows me to roam freely at my will…And when I move from a town, the cat that I brought with me, I leave there. That way it doesn't raise any suspicion when they don't see a black cat running around anymore… I have things that need to be done before my move tomorrow."

Monty stopped the recording. "That's everything."

"People thought they saw Magic running around town, but it was really her as a werecat?" asked Gwyn.

"Yes, I believe so," replied Monty. "Magic, for a better word, was her decoy."

"What ever happened to the moving truck?" asked Andrew.

"I checked with the local moving companies, and none of them had her booked for that morning, or any time after that."

"That's strange," suggested Andrew.

"She was a strange woman," declared Monty.

"Well, I would have never suspected her," said Gwyn shaking her head in disbelief.

"Me neither," admitted Andrew. "Do you think she wanted people to know what she was up to?"

"My theory is that she did, some individuals that are unbalanced, tend to want to leave their creepy legacy behind."

"But she seemed so normal to me," said Gwyn.

"A lot of people like her act that way, but deep down they have another side to them, a hidden, darker side," said Monty.

Magic meowed behind the screen door, Andrew opened it, and watched him as he jumped onto Gwyn's lap.

"Magic was lucky he was at Andrew's when the fire happened," she said caressing him.

"He was," confirmed Monty reaching over and stroking him. "I see you got him a collar."

"Yes, we did, we picked one up for him when we took him for a checkup yesterday," replied Gwyn. "The vet said he is doing fine."

"That's good, poor fella's been through a lot."

"He has, but we'll take good care of him."

"I'm sure you will," said Monty with a kind smile, then leaned back in his seat, looked over at Andrew, and collected his thoughts before he spoke. "Inside the filing cabinet, I also found duplicates of the flash drive and documents you gave me."

"I guess we now know who the owner of the original files was," stated Andrew.

"We do," said Monty nodding his head. "Along with those, was a twenty-five-page binder. Each page in the binder contained a list of names, and at the top of the page, the town they were from. The first page was the most recent, and it was the names of the victims from Thornton. We also found soft copies of those lists, and their accompanying spreadsheets, on her laptop, but nothing else. I did contact a couple of the towns, and they confirmed that the individuals I had inquired about, had died accidentally or mysteriously. I asked if there were any traces of a cat being present at the crime scenes, they confirmed there was."

"Are you saying what I think you are?" asked Andrew.

"I know," he replied scratching his head, "I have a difficult time believing it myself. But there is a strong possibility, that Lenore, not only turned into a cat and killed people in Thornton but had previously done so in other towns."

Andrew and Gwyn quickly glanced at one another.

"Again, that's just my take," clarified Monty.

"We understand," said Andrew.

"So, what's next?" asked Gwyn.

"Nothing," said Monty. "As far as Thornton is concerned, they were all accidents, and the investigation is closed."

"Accidents?" asked Andrew.

"Lenore is dead," he replied, "and if she was the reason behind these so-called accidents, then there won't be anymore. Therefore, she's no longer a threat to Thornton or any other town."

"In her recording, she said she was the last of her kind, did she have any family?" asked Gwyn.

"I did a background check on her, to see if she had any surviving relatives to inform of her passing. Unfortunately, she had none. In fact, she had quite a sad life. Her father died of cancer when she was very young. And when she was in her early twenties, her mother Eleanor Peabody, was allegedly raped and murdered by three men. At the trial, the defense lawyer painted a picture of her mother as being a witch, who practiced witchcraft and black magic, and liked having group sex. With witness testimonies to back up his allegations, eyewitness accounts, and insufficient evidence, the jury found the men not guilty, and they were set free. After that, Lenore moved to Plymouth, where she lived with her grandparents, then to Sandwich to stay with her aunt and uncle, before moving out on her own."

"She said she lived in those places, but she never told us anything about her background," acknowledged Andrew.

"From what I understand, she was a private woman when it came to her past."

"What happened to her is such a shame," said Gwyn, feeling a little sorry for the young Lenore.

"It is, but it still doesn't make it right, to do what she did to all those people, whether they deserved it or not," stated Monty slowly standing, putting on his hat, and glancing over at the remnants. "The town is knocking down what's left of that structure on Monday and removing the debris. Then the landowner is going to start to build a new house," said Monty turning to them, "and all this will be behind us for good."

Gwyn and Andrew looked at him silently.

"Have a nice afternoon."

"You too," replied Andrew.

"Thanks, we will," said Gwyn.

Monty started for the steps, stopped, and looked back at them deciding whether to say something or not. "There was one odd document I found."

"What was that?" asked Andrew.

"It was 'Grandma's Secret Chocolate Chip Cookie Recipe.'"

"That is odd!" said Gwyn. "Why would that be there?"

"I thought the same thing," said Monty. "So, I went online to see if any of the ingredients were unusual."

"Thinking maybe it was a potion for a spell?" asked Gwyn trying not to laugh.

"Something like that," replied Monty snickering at himself for thinking such a thing. "Seems there are dozens of 'Grandma's Secret Chocolate Chip Cookie Recipes' to choose from, most of them with the same ingredients."

"I do remember her bringing those cookies to the church hall one evening," recalled Gwyn mischievously, "and they were quite delicious, weren't they Andrew?"

"Yes, they were," he confirmed giving her a smile, then glancing over at Monty. "What was your take on the recipe?"

"Quite simple really, she was mocking me and the department with it," he replied.

"What did you do with it?" asked Andrew.

"Last night, I had a bonfire with the wife and kids in the backyard, and threw it in. I don't think we need to be reminded of her taunting and ridiculing us anymore."

"Definitely not," agreed Andrew.

They watched the deputy sheriff start down the steps, stop, and turn around.

"The only thing that was missing from that filing cabinet was a big red bow around it," he said with a smile.

"I think you nailed it earlier, when you said she wanted to leave her creepy legacy behind," said Andrew. "She's left everything in that filing cabinet for you to find, hoping that you would go public with it, but I'm guessing you won't be giving her that satisfaction?"

"No way!" replied Monty steadfastly. "This case is closed, and what I found in that filing cabinet, will never see the light of day."

"That's what I thought," said Andrew.

Monty looked at the burnt-down house, then at Andrew and Gwyn. "I'm guessing Lenore's accident will be the last?"

Gwyn quickly glanced over at Andrew.

"With what you have shared with us today, it sounds like you have definitely found the person responsible, and I believe hers will be the last," stated Andrew.

"Me too," said Monty convinced.

"As long as we don't see any more stray black cats," joked Gwyn.

"I don't think we will," replied the deputy sheriff with a chuckle. "And remember, everything we just talked about, is all—"

"Unofficial!" they replied and laughed.

He smiled at them, walked down to his cruiser, then waved goodbye before jumping in, and driving away.

"I told you we should have put a red bow on it!" said Gwyn looking at him.

"Well, figuratively, we did," replied Andrew with a smile.

"What do you want to do now?"

Andrew thought momentarily. "How about a nice dinner with a bottle of wine followed by a leisurely stroll into town?"

"I'd like that," she replied, putting Magic on the porch swing, and standing.

Chapter Twenty-Six

"That cookie recipe wasn't your grandma's?" asked Andrew as they walked down Liberty Street.

"Of course not," replied Gwyn with a giggle. "I even gave you an odd look when you asked me to type my grandma's recipe ingredients."

"You did," said Andrew recalling her reaction.

"Besides, even if she had a secret cookie recipe, I wouldn't give it up just like that," she said snapping her fingers. "The one I typed; I just remembered it from the internet."

Andrew shook his head. "You're something else."

"I know, aren't I," she replied with an adorable smile, then gave him a mysterious look. "But my grandma does have one great secret recipe."

"Oh really! What would that be?"

"My 'Grandma Blunt's Chocolate Cake Recipe,'" she said proudly.

"Now, that's a recipe you never want to share," admitted Andrew. "That cake was divine!"

"How about tomorrow, we make one together, just for us?"

"You're going to share your family's secret recipe with me?" he asked slowing down and stopping.

"Grandma said I should only share it with cherished ones," confirmed Gwyn walking back to him.

Andrew drew her close and kissed her tenderly. After they parted, Gwyn grabbed his hand, and they continued their walk.

"Where do you want to go?" she asked beaming.

"Either The Olde Towne Fool or Daisy's?" suggested Andrew.

"The Olde Towne Fool first, then Daisy's, and inside each place, I'm going to give you a long, passionate kiss, right in front of everyone," she confirmed happily.

"To give the townspeople something spicy to mouth about?"

"Exactly!" she replied, then suddenly stopped, moved close to him, and kissed him devotedly. Her heart fluttered as she gazed deeply into his eyes. "I'm in love with you."

Andrew smiled and kissed her gently on the lips. "I love you," he declared as his fingers softly caressed her cheek.

She liked his gentle touch, and before he moved his hand away, she took it, kissed it affectionately, and then held it. "We make a pretty good team," she whispered.

"We do," he said quietly.

"I think we did a great job of wrapping everything up."

"Yes, we did. Maybe next time, I'll buy you a big red bow to put on the evidence."

Gwyn giggled. "Next time," she repeated, "that sounds nice." Then realized what she was saying. "Wait a minute! I hope there is no next time!"

"I'm sure there won't be," said Andrew laughing with her.

"Now that it's officially over, can I ask you something?"

"Of course, anything."

"Back at the diner, and knowing you, probably before that, how did you know the cat was involved?"

He looked at her reflectively. "I don't know, I've always had a knack for seeing things…differently."

"So, you're a weirdo?" she teased.

Andrew chuckled. "I must be if I'm with you!"

"Why you fucker!" she replied and tried to move away.

Andrew pulled her back, kissed her full on the mouth, and she responded fervently. When they eventually stopped, he put his arm around her and she placed hers around his waist, and then cuddled into his shoulder as they amorously strolled arm in arm to The Olde Towne Fool.

"Inside, there's something I need to talk to you about, and hopefully with your skills, you can help me out," said Andrew opening the door.

"My skills," she said curiously.

They went past the bar, looked around, and found a secluded booth in the back.

"This must be something important," she said noticing his expression.

"I'm not sure," he replied. "Chances are, it's probably nothing."

Gwyn laughed. "Andrew, if there's one thing I learnt from being around you, there's no such thing as a 'chances are, it's probably nothing.'"

"We definitely hang out too much!"

They ordered drinks from the waitress, and waited till she dropped them off, before talking.

"There was something Monty said earlier, that reminded me of an item I found in one of my great-uncle's personal effects boxes."

"What?" asked Gwyn eagerly leaning forward.

"Inside one of them, was a shoebox containing personal letters and cards, and also a small box of four by six photos of family and friends. There was one picture I studied in particular, because at the time it seemed odd, but I didn't give it any more thought, until today."

"Odd, how?"

Andrew removed the picture from his pocket then passed it to Gwyn. "That's my mom and dad on either side of my great-uncle."

"They all look very happy," she said glancing up at him. "What's odd about it?"

"The picture was taken in the fall, look outside the window behind them, it's a beautiful sunny day."

"You're wondering why they are in a bedroom?"

"Yes, that's the spare bedroom where I slept, where we sleep. They could have taken that picture in the living room, on the porch, in the front yard, or by the oak tree out back."

"Maybe it's because they knew you slept there, and it would make you feel like they were there with you, you know, in spirit."

Andrew gave her a dubious look.

"All right, enough with the look already," she said chuckling, "you want my analytical side, not my sensitive one."

"Actually, your computer-nerdy side!"

"You keep that up and you'll be sleeping alone in this room tonight," she said glancing up at him and tapping the photo on her free hand, before looking back down at it. "I don't know, there is something peculiar about your mom…about her pose."

Andrew took the picture from her and looked at it. "She's just leaning into my great-uncle, and her body is naturally sloping that way."

"No," said Gwyn unconvinced. "She looks awkward…wait, no…not awkward…she looks intentional."

"Intentional," repeated Andrew studying the photo momentarily, then glancing up. "There's also writing on the back," he said handing it to her. "The date the picture was taken, which was three months before they died, and a comment."

Gwyn sympathetically squeezed his hand, then read it. "Andrew, after this was taken, I joked with your mom about how she used to say, 'when one case is closed, another one appears right under your feet,' making her laugh – she loved her Nancy Drew TV show." Gwyn glanced up confused, then looked down at the writing, and noticed something about the ink. "This comment was written much later, not at the same time as the date. In fact, I would say within the last couple of months."

"You've just confirmed what I thought," said Andrew. "But there's something else, my mom never watched Nancy Drew, it was always the Hardy Boys."

"Did your great-uncle make a mistake?"

"Not a chance, he always teased her by saying she married my dad because he was a sleuth, like the Hardy Boys."

"So, he intentionally made that error, to bring your attention to something," said Gwyn thinking out loud, her mind now turning. "It's definitely not about him teasing her, it's about her, her and this comment."

Andrew was silent, allowing Gwyn's instincts to take over.

"When one case is closed, when one case is closed," she repeated, then something came to her, she glanced up at Andrew. "Today, Monty said the case was closed, which is what you were alluding to earlier, so that's already happened, that's not the clue." She looked at the rest of the comment. "Another one appears right under your feet," she said quietly, then flipped over to the photo, studied it, then looked up at him excitedly. "I've got it!"

Andrew smiled at her.

"Wait a minute," she said sitting back, "you knew I would figure this out."

"Maybe, but once a nerd always a—"

"Do not finish that sentence, or else!"

"Or else, what?" he asked egging her on with a comical face.

"Trust me, you don't want to find out, mister!" responded Gwyn playfully, then got out of her seat, sat next to him, and shared the photo. "Now, look at your mom, at her body language."

"I still don't notice anything," he admitted.

"Here, let me help you. Just follow the right side of her body, as it intentionally slopes all the way down to her extended foot, which is..."

"Pointing to the rug on the floor," finished Andrew, then quickly glanced up at Gwyn. "Which means there is something hidden underneath the floorboard."

"Yes!" she said ecstatically. "And do you remember when we bought the basket for Magic, and we put it in the corner of the bedroom, but he wouldn't sleep in it?"

"Yeah," he replied, "we thought he preferred sleeping on the rug."

"And what did you do?"

"I put the basket on the part of the rug where he liked to sleep, and he slept in it."

"Which is the exact spot your mom's foot is pointing to!" declared Gwyn happily.

They downed their drinks, quickly walked home, and went upstairs to the bedroom.

"There he is, protecting something," commented Gwyn, as she watched Andrew pick up the basket with Magic curled up inside, and place it in the corner.

With Magic in tow, Andrew joined Gwyn by the rug, and knelt next to her. As he lifted it up and folded it in half, Magic excitedly purred and rubbed up against him.

"He knows something's under there," said Gwyn moving Magic out of Andrew's way.

Andrew quickly scanned the area and noticed that four floorboards were cut into a rectangular shape and attached. He found a small hole in one of them, put his index finger inside, lifted it up, and placed the floorboard aside. Then reached in, removed a heavy cardboard box, and placed it in the middle of the room. He nervously looked over at Gwyn, "the moment of truth," he said. Then opened the box, removed an item covered in a baby's blanket, and placed it in between them. Andrew unfolded the blanket and revealed a very old and heavy gray book with a pentacle on its cover."

"Oh my God!" exclaimed Gwyn. "It's a grimoire!"

"Grimoire?" asked Andrew looking at her.

"A witch's spell book."

Andrew looked down, slowly opened it, and read the title, "The Gray Witches." He flipped through the pages, passing spell after spell. When he got closer to the middle, there were numerous blank pages. Suddenly, a page with a list of eleven names, written in ink and dating back to the 18th century, appeared.

Gwyn looked at the names closely, turned the page and looked at those names, then the next page, then the next, before going back to the first. "It's a genealogy," said Gwyn looking up at him. "Each person on this first page has one relative on the next page, then that relative is related to one person on the following page, and so on. I'm guessing a person is the parent, and the relative on the following page, is their son or daughter."

"So, these names on this first page are the parent of a child on the second page, the grandparent of a child on the third page, the great-grandparent of a child on the fourth page, and so on, till we get to the last page?"

"Yes," confirmed Gwyn, "these first names, are the ancestors of the last names entered."

Andrew quickly flipped to the second to last page, looked at the first name, and pointed it out to Gwyn.

"Sophia Henderson-Blake," she said glancing up at Andrew. "Is that your mother?"

"It must be, my mother's maiden name is Henderson," he replied, turning the page.

Gwyn read the first name, looked up at him, and slowly whispered, "I don't believe it, Andrew Blake!"

"Yes," he replied stunned.

"This means that your mother was a Gray Witch and—"

"I am the son of a Gray Witch."

"That would explain your…gifts?"

"Something like that," he replied, and glanced down at the second name, flipped back a page, reviewed it, then looked over at Gwyn.

"What?" she asked detecting his stare.

"Speaking of gifts," he said. "Did you ever think you had any?"

Gwyn laughed. "Me? No, not at all."

Andrew suddenly went serious. "Really? You believed a stray black cat was possessed."

"No, I didn't, I thought it was bullshit!"

"I'm talking later on, when you told Monty in his office."

Gwyn thought back. "Okay, yeah, maybe I did. So?"

"By manipulating data and using bar charts, you figured out a way of deciphering the information on the spreadsheet, and how Lenore was attaining it."

"Yeah, but come on, I learnt that at my summer job."

"You also questioned me several times about the 'Ailuranthropy' book Lenore had."

Gwyn went silent.

"When I told you my plan about setting Lenore's place on fire, you said—"

"A fire is the only way we can kill her, a malevolent witch."

"You figured out the clue on the photo my great-uncle left me."

"Andrew, you're starting to scare me."

"And you knew what this book was as soon as you saw it."

"I did," she said nervously.

"Have you ever seen one before?"

"No."

"And just like that," he said snapping his fingers, "you told me it contained the genealogy of eleven families, dating back from the 18th century, right up until the last names entered. Would you consider all this, normal behavior for you?"

"No, it's not."

"Then you could say they are out of character, perhaps, hidden gifts."

"Enough Andrew, please stop, you're frightening me."

"Is your mother's maiden name, Spencer, as in Mary Spencer-Blunt?"

"How the fuck did you know that?"

Andrew pointed to the second name, on the second to last page.

"Mary Spencer-Blunt," read Gwyn, then slowly turned the page, "Gwyneth Blunt." She quickly glanced over at Andrew. "I'm the fucking daughter of a Gray Witch!" she said anxiously standing and pacing around the room, while Magic animatedly purred and rubbed his back against her. She suddenly stopped and looked down at him. "Magic knew about us all along, didn't he?"

"I'm guessing so."

"That's why he wanted to be around us all the time," she said bending down, stroking him, and glancing over at Andrew. "Do you remember Lenore saying that the way Magic acted around us we could be witches?"

"I do."

"Do you think she thought that maybe we were? Or even knew that we were?"

"I don't know…I don't think so."

"Either way, with Magic wanting to be around us constantly, he almost blew our cover," suggested Gwyn looking down at him. "Very soon we are going to have to give you a stern talking to, young man, won't we Andrew?"

"Yes, we will," he replied smiling at her.

Gwyn managed a smile back.

"Look on the bright side. We solved the murders, gave all the evidence to the deputy sheriff, left no loose ends, and nobody suspects who we are."

"Not even us!" said Gwyn making them laugh. "I guess secrecy is 'our' best ally."

"Yes, it is."

"Are there any other surprises?" teased Gwyn sitting next to him.

"There is one more," replied Andrew hesitantly.

"I was joking!"

"Then please, hold onto your sense of humor, you'll need it."

"Why am I getting this awful feeling that I'm not going to like this one bit?"

"You probably won't."

Andrew stood up, walked over to his black bag and picked it up, then sat back next to Gwyn. "Do you remember at Lenore's when we were putting the books and documents in the fireproof cabinet?"

"I do."

"When I went back to get the binder from the bookshelf, as I pulled it out, a key fell."

"Key, what key?"

"It was for the cabinet drawer underneath" he replied. "So, before I left, I opened it, removed its wrapped contents, and placed it in this bag."

"What the fuck is it?" she said sensing something bad.

"I don't know, I haven't seen it yet, and wanted to look at it with you."

"Andrew, going for a walk, watching a movie, lying in bed, that's what I want you to do with me. Not unwrap some creepy artifact from a crazy dead witch's house."

"Do you want to leave?" he asked playfully motioning to the door.

"Nice try, but you know me better than that, and already know my answer, so let's get on with it."

Andrew unzipped the bag and took out an item covered in a baby's blanket.

"Oh shit!" said Gwyn. "This does not look good!"

Andrew unfolded the blanket and they both stared down at a black grimoire with a pentacle on it. He turned to the first page, there was a white envelope, so he picked it up then read the book title, "The Black Witches."

"No fucking way!" said Gwyn in a low voice.

Andrew looked at the envelope and read it, "For Salem."

"What the fuck!"

He opened it, took out three photos, and studied them before handing them to Gwyn.

Gwyn slowly looked at them, then nervously at Andrew. "Are you fucking kidding me?"

About the Author

Edgar Waldgrave lives in

the small, quaint town of Skaneateles,

Onondaga County, New York.

You can contact him on his website:

www.edgarwaldgrave.com

Or on Facebook:

Edgar Waldgrave